ENJOY SUCCESS, RELISH FAILURES

A.D. Padmasingh Isaac is the founder and managing director of Aachi Masala Foods Pvt. Ltd, a ₹1,000-crore-plus company (www.aachifoods.com), which he founded in 1996. It directly employs around 3,500 people in its various manufacturing facilities in Ayanambakkam and Gummidipoondi, Chennai. Mr Isaac worked in the early 1980s for Godrej Consumer Products. As a first-generation entrepreneur he went through a good deal of struggle before he established the Aachi brand. The Aachi Masala brand is quite popular in South India. He is a motivational speaker in many youth fora and holds advisory responsibilities in the Indian Institute of Crop Processing Technology, Thanjavur, and the National Institute of Food Technology Entrepreneurship and Management (NIFTEM), Haryana.

ENJOY SUCCESS, RELISH FAILURES

A.D. PADMASINGH ISAAC

RUPA

Published by
Rupa Publications India Pvt. Ltd 2019
7/16, Ansari Road, Daryaganj
New Delhi 110002

Sales centres:
Allahabad Bengaluru Chennai
Hyderabad Jaipur Kathmandu
Kolkata Mumbai

The views and opinions expressed in this book are the author's own and the facts
are as reported by him/her which have been verified to the extent possible, and the
publishers are not in any way liable for the same.

ISBN: 978-93-5333-784-1

First impression 2019

10 9 8 7 6 5 4 3 2 1

The moral right of the author has been asserted.

I dedicate this book to all my customers, my Aachi family…

I began in a humble way, with the purpose of giving my customers the best of taste, quality and health. Soon, they welcomed Aachi into their households. They have made us their great kitchen partners! It's a lifelong relationship to cherish. I'm ever thankful to my customers.

CONTENTS

FOREWORD

It gives me great joy to write the foreword to Padmasingh Isaac's book because I consider it an honour to do so for a book written by a man who is the very definition of the word 'entrepreneur'. He has been relentless in his endeavour to create the brand Aachi Masala, against all odds. Through everything, he has kept his eye on the goal with single-minded focus, and continued on his journey till he got to the point where he is today. In this book, he describes his journey with great honesty. For example, he describes how at one point in his journey when he almost hit rock-bottom, he was forced to pledge his wife's mangalsutra to save his business. Such anecdotes would resonate with many entrepreneurs in India, as many had to resort to extreme measures to stay afloat.

As I read through the manuscript, there was a sense of déjà vu, as he described the tough journey an entrepreneur invariably goes through in the start-up days. I had experienced many similar situations while building GoodKnight. Since at that time, it was a novel concept in India, it was challenging: the concept of protection from mosquitoes without smoke and smearing cream on the body. Our customers were initially apprehensive about accepting a liquid vaporizer as a repellent. On many instances, our efforts were rejected, but I was convinced that we were doing the right thing and kept our eye squarely on the goal of building a world-class brand that would make India proud. There were many people who were waiting to see if we were going to fail and, like Padmasingh, we continued working hard to prove the naysayers wrong. Through all the hardships and less-than-ideal experiences on our business journey, we persisted and managed to create a national brand. I am able to put myself in Padmasingh's shoes and empathize with his experiences, whether hardships or celebrations!

In this book, Padmasingh wants readers to relish failures first, as they are inevitable and every entrepreneur would have failed on some occasion or the other. When facing failures, it is very important to never allow the spirit to break and think less of one's abilities. I agree with him when he says, 'You have to believe in yourself first.' That's the first step in motivating oneself to face failures, learn from mistakes and rise to achieve success. The many narratives of his business experiences are sure to hold the rapt attention of readers.

When Padmasingh speaks about the success that he has achieved, he mentions that one should not rest on one's laurels but continue to work hard. He explains the struggles a butterfly goes through before becoming a 'thing of beauty', while insisting that such laurels would only come to people who continuously toil with the welfare of others in mind. And it is indeed true that one ought not to stop toiling and continue to adopt the readiness to do hard work always.

This book, written in a simple and evocative style, carries a number of analogies and allusions which make it an interesting read. Saying that this book will provide the reader with management lessons is selling it short; I would say that this book gives all of us life lessons and provides us with the faith that hard work, determination and a never-say-die attitude truly do pay off in the end.

Every budding and established entrepreneur must read Padmasingh's book. It carries his indelible footprints that one can follow, to walk the path of true success.

A. Mahendran
Chairman and managing director,
Global Consumer Products Pvt. Ltd, Mumbai
Former managing director,
Godrej Consumer Products Ltd

PREFACE

My entrepreneurial journey is punctuated with many incidents and events, both good and bad. They can be relished, as well as enjoyed. I have learnt many things through each of my experiences. Samuel L. Clemens, the American writer and humorist, known by his pen name Mark Twain, calls his whimsically written autobiography a 'combined diary and autography'. My writings about my entrepreneurial journey are collated and drawn from the notes I had jotted down in my diary. They are shared in an informal but didactic manner, to encourage budding entrepreneurs.

The learning that I have gained from my immediate family, my school and college life, my career and my entrepreneurial journey has made me who I am today: the person who has created an organization that has been helpful to everyone in its ecosystem. In that context, this book carries the true experiences of my learning process. The takeaways from this book can be, I feel, a beacon to our youth, the future of our nation. This book could become valuable orientation material for entering a new world of entrepreneurship and business management. Thus, my business journey is recorded with this purpose in mind, and not merely as a recounting of my life's experiences, which traces the hard trials of failures and the pain gone through to achieve success.

The Aachi Group of companies buys tonnes of agricultural products from all over India, benefitting lakhs of farmers. When these are converted into quality food products, millions of people are benefitted. Many workers are employed, either directly or indirectly. Through this, thousands of families are supported. The products sell across millions of shops, benefitting many shopkeepers. Since our products are exported, the government's exchequer receives large amounts of revenue through foreign exchange. Similarly, many businessmen contribute greatly towards the economic improvement of our nation. Their failures and successes impact society to a large extent. Hence, the life stories of businessmen could be more significant than even those of politicians!

It is a dream of mine that more and more businessmen contribute to the development of our nation. If one takes the first step to becoming a businessman, one becomes a leader. There's a dire need today for role models and this presents an opportunity to the right person. Without proper role models, the wrong ones are often chosen!

Once you're a successful businessman and become a leader, society is transformed through you. This is a transformation that has the potential to better people's health, lifespan, education, economy and equality. It could impact every aspect of living. That is why I have made this book available to you, with every intention of seeing you become a successful businessman and an impactful leader!

Many of you who've understood my intentions will also wonder why we need to face hurdles that lie ahead in the process of becoming a successful businessman. I can almost hear people saying, 'Without money, there is nothing!' I agree that money is needed. But, please understand that money, by itself, has not performed any miracles in the world.

The founder of Infosys, N.R. Narayana Murthy was born to an ordinary school teacher in Mysore. He was one of nine children. He completed his schooling from a government school, received his Bachelor of Engineering (BE) degree and started his career as a computer programmer. When he was thirty years old, he started a company called Softronics, which ended in a huge loss. He closed down his business and found a job for himself. After five years, in 1981, he started his entrepreneurship journey again. This time, all he invested was Rs 10,000 provided by his wife Sudha Murthy from her savings.

Dhirubhai Ambani too was born to a school teacher in a hamlet in Gujarat. Not able to finish his college studies, he went to Yemen to work. On his return, he started a business with an investment of Rs 15,000. That was the foundation of the internationally famous Reliance Group.

I have quoted these two examples to prove that money is not an absolute requisite for becoming a businessman. A small amount of capital is enough to start most businesses.

Next, you may cite 'fear of failure' as a hurdle.

Thomas Alva Edison, who was deeply involved in scientific inventions till the age of eighty, held patents for 1,093 inventions. When he was asked, 'How many times have you failed to succeed?' He replied, 'Failures are as honourable as success. I can never find the thing that does the job best until I find the ones that don't. So, I have not failed. Rather, I have just found ten thousand ways that won't work.' That is, ten thousand wrong findings (failures) have paved the way to the correct results. Realizing that failure is a lesson or an experience, he continued with his efforts and invented thousands of things. So, take steps without any fear of failure!

The same Edison encouraged relentless pursuers, saying, 'Our greatest weakness lies in giving up. Many of life's failures are people who never realized how close they were to success when they gave up. The most certain way to succeed is always to try just one more time.'

The reason behind compiling my experiences and learning is to put together the broken bits of my 'failures' and see how I succeeded through them, taking each failure as a stepping stone to reach the goals set by me, time and time again.

Failures were always around me and attacked me from all sides; I felt ashamed and deeply hurt; rejected by friends and relatives, the hurdles shook me very often, even as worries and dejection tried to oppress me. I faced so many disappointments, but I plodded on.

If you are being pulled down by failure, or feeling hurt or ashamed, or if you have been rejected by friends and relatives or find yourself hindered in all your efforts even as you are oppressed by disappointments, then this is the book for you. In this book, I have charted a plan for you to fight against all odds without losing heart and to strive for success.

Here you will see the path drawn by me, an ordinary man. I have walked on this path for more than forty years and have found success. There's no doubt that you will get many tips from me here to help you on your journey to success.

While I was writing this book, I had the opportunity to discuss my thoughts with my friend and former colleague, Dr Gibson G. Vedamani, who gladly shared his insights and case examples that I have added to make this book even more interesting.

As you read through my experiences, my hope is that it will inspire you to strive towards even greater success in your life!

A.D. Padmasingh Isaac

1

LEARNING TO BELIEVE IN MYSELF

I grew up in Nazareth.

Nazareth! What powerful images this name conjures—of a young carpenter from the biblical days, who went from hammering nails to being hammered to death on a cross, but not before changing the world around him, and the world that came to be. The Nazareth that I was born is in Tuticorin, Tamil Nadu, though not very different from the other one! Laid-back, insignificant, rustic, it had all the poverty our country offers. It would have remained the same, had it not been blessed again by a man of God. It was Canon Arthur Margoschis who decided to concentrate his life and efforts on not just the spiritual development of his parishioners but also on the development of the area.

From a Sleepy Village to a Modern Town

It was named after the original Nazareth because here too were the beginnings of the evangelical work which had later spread across the rest of the country. With such a historical connection,

I always felt a sense of positivity coming out of this humble place of my birth, a positivity that helped me in much of my innovative thinking.

But before I get into that, let me tell you more about this town to which I owe a lot. The early 1800s saw the arrival of a number of evangelists from across the seas whose sole intention was to change the world through social change. And that change, as I said earlier, was through education, hygiene and healthcare. The man instrumental in all this was Canon Arthur Margoschis. By the time I was born, this little town, with the slow rumbling of age-old bullock carts and the timelessness that all Indian villages have, also had schools and hygienic surroundings, quite unusual for many Indian villages. And it was this that set the town of Nazareth quite apart!

The opening of one's mind comes through education. Education, in our little Nazareth, started first with a primary school set up by these same worthy and dedicated personnel from the Western world. A middle school, vocational institutions and other institutions of training, were established too. As with all things, basic education was followed by homes created for destitute men and women. Churches and a hospital soon joined the other buildings in the town. Recognition of the rapid growth of the town was seen in the establishment of a post office and a grocery store, and with these came town planning, and the restructuring of the streets of what was once a sleepy little village.

Nazareth Uses Its Own Resources

With all these changes, Nazareth had surely come into its own and I, for one, always reiterate that I was fortunate to have been born in a town like this. But I'm sure that there are many of you who wonder how Nazareth fared economically. Most villages in the country grow around a water body, like a pond or a lake. But Nazareth had no such luxury, no pond for irrigation, and also no canals built to bring water from the rivers. But what we had were palmyra trees! This tree, apart from being the official tree of the state, is a hardy, water-retaining tree, and was the source of agricultural income for the people of my town.

There's much that this tree gives and much that we made use of: jaggery and palm sugar were exported, leaf stem peels were used for weaving the base of furniture and traditional cots, the tree trunks were used as reapers for the construction of houses, the leaves for making hand-fans, while dried palmyra leaves were used for roofing our thatched huts. In a town which often faced drought situations, this evergreen tree provided round-the-year income and even contributed to exports, enhancing the government's exchequer. I write in depth about this tree to show how, like my ancestors, one can make different uses of already available resources and with one's creativity, in order to be able to look after one's financial needs.

Family Bonding

Now that you know a little about where I grew up, let me introduce you to my immediate family. Within a few months of his marriage, my father Devasahayam Isaac accompanied my grandfather Asirvatham Nadar to Colombo, in erstwhile Ceylon (now Sri Lanka), on business. While the business was thriving, my grandfather who was just fifty-one years old, unfortunately passed away, leaving my young father to shoulder the responsibilities of home, hearth and business. But my father, instead of bemoaning his fate, moved wholeheartedly into his new responsibility and started working industriously.

When I look back, I imagine that it could have only been my father's example of entrepreneurial willingness that also gave me the courage to give up a steady job and venture into business. I not only embraced a new adventure, but learnt from scratch, the basics of branding and marketing a consumer product. The targets that I had to meet made me think out of the box, and there's no doubt that it was the example of my forefathers that gave me the ability to excel.

Working for Others, Works Well for You

It was the evangelist, Canon Arthur Margoschis, who believed and spread his view that education, hygiene, spiritualism and healthcare, packaged together, would lead to societal well-being. And this was aptly seen in my hometown Nazareth, which was well-developed in education and culture, owing to his efforts and of the others who came with him and after him. It was also during this time in the 1990s that education, culture and development began to take root in several parts of Tamil Nadu. In Nazareth, as I have mentioned earlier, the establishment of a primary school grew, with time, into a middle school, which led to the need for vocational educational institutions, training institutes, a Bible college, a home for the destitute and even a hospital to cater to the growing medical needs of the people. Modernization made its entry in the form of these new beginnings that restructured the streets of Nazareth.

It fascinated me that someone like Margoschis could make a huge impact by developing the society around him, and working to provide for the various needs of people around him. He made a difference to society, and this made me think about the ways in which I could also make a difference, in my own way.

Even as I started believing in myself, I realized that building a virtuous and disciplined environment, first at home and then at school, as well as the beautiful effects of family bonding and love, could take one to great heights.

Discipline and Love: A Lovely Combination

I'm sure you'll agree that home is the first school for any child, just as much as parents are the first teachers and role models. My parents had one intention and that was to educate us and thus make us beneficial to society at large. In the process, they came to believe that discipline was a very important criterion for this and, thus, we were brought up to be highly disciplined.

Now, let's talk about family love and bonding. Though my father left for Colombo to continue the business of my grandfather, he used to visit Nazareth once in every two years. But, though far away, he gave us the feeling that he was very close to us. He did this through the gifts that he brought back for all of us like clothes, jewels and snacks, which made us realize how much he loved all of us, and made us understand that our father actually missed us and yearned to spend more time with us. This taught us the value of a happy family life and its importance in a person's life.

Also, during his stay at Nazareth, I used to observe the way he helped and supported my mother in the field and with the cattle. Watching him made me learn at quite a tender age that women need to be loved, respected and their responsibilities shared by their spouses. I also learnt about faith and observed that their unshakeable faith in God sowed the seeds of spiritualism in me and my siblings. Our parents instilled in us the need to inculcate patience, dedication, righteousness, self-confidence and compassion as the foundation of our deep-rooted value system.

The Strength of a Woman

And then, catastrophe struck when my father passed away suddenly.

His death was a dreadful blow to the family. But, in the process, I learnt a lot from the way my mother handled the tragic situation. I saw that showing compassion despite her tragedy, as well as showing respect to others helped, as she took on the mantle of leadership.

As I observed my mother during this period, I saw how important money management was, and the importance of savings and investment in the form of jewellery or livestock to meet unforeseen contingencies. These were very valuable lessons that I learnt while I was young. I saw the hard work put in by my mother after the sudden demise of my father, which made me understand that there is no substitute for hard work and I also saw how hard work always pays off in the long run. After my father passed away, my mother was always careful to ensure that we never felt our father's absence and showered us with a double dose of love.

There is much that I admire in my mother: her boldness, positivity, administrative skills, presence of mind and ability to bounce back after a setback. Her ability to hide her difficulties from others and never lose an opportunity to help the needy is commendable. All this made me realize, more than ever, that I should lead my life along similar lines. Today, I am proud to say that all that I am, I owe to my mother, who was and is my role model.

She had no formal education and was suddenly faced with the burden of providing for six children. I must mention here that her faith in God and her practice of using uplifting words from the Bible gave her immense confidence and resolve to face the challenges that cropped up. As we watched her, we learnt lessons that have helped us live, especially the way she made huge sacrifices to make both ends meet. Despite all these troubles, when her sister passed away leaving behind three children, my mother did not hesitate to bring them up along with us and, again, what impressed me was the equal treatment she gave them. This made me realize that equality, patience and compassion form the basis of a successful person. Now, looking back, I realize what I hardly did then—that my mother had all the qualities of a successful leader and could influence others with her care and concern.

Catastrophes and Self-belief

There were many lessons that I learnt from my mother and I knew right at the beginning that she certainly believed in herself. When my father was in Colombo, he used to send Rs 30 or 50 every month. Do remember that this was seventy years ago, but with that money my mother met all our expenses and also managed to save. At that time, we had five cows and calves at home. My mother would get up at five in the morning and milk the cows. She also reared sheep and fowls. All this kept her extremely busy. This is where I learnt not just about hard work, but also about patience and self-confidence. The unexpected death of my father shook the very roots of our family. A lot of money was needed to educate and support six children and, realizing this, my mother would get up early in the morning, milk the cows and sell the milk. She then collected the eggs laid by our hens, saw to the welfare of the sheep and went to the market to sell the eggs. She taught us the principle 'whatever the expenses, it can be met by hard work and not by borrowing'. My mother was the personification of determined resolve and infinite patience.

My mother never lied. Here, I must recount an incident: Once, we went with her by car, to attend a wedding. The driver was drunk and we were involved in an accident, though we managed to escape with slight injuries. Unfortunately, a pedestrian was killed. My mother was adamant and told us, 'The one who did wrong should be punished and the victim should get justice and financial compensation.' With that, she stood as a witness and testified against her driver in court. As a result, the victim's family got the compensation that they deserved. From this incident, I learnt about justice, integrity and courage.

My mother was also the epitome of compassion. Even though she was burdened with the responsibility of looking after three children of her own, she had no second thoughts in taking on the responsibility and caring for her late sister's children, treating them as her very own.

She was also fearless. Sometimes, late in the night when the cows or hens made strange noises, perhaps on seeing a snake, she would walk out into the darkness to see what the problem was. Time and again, she proved to us that women are bolder than men.

When I look back, I realize how the death of my father took us from the comforts of a life of rural luxury to unexpected sorrows and hardships. This sudden stormy weather could have destroyed our family which had never experienced difficulties or worries till that time. My mother, then forty-six years old, braved the storm. I was fifteen years old and in the tenth standard at St Margoschis School. My elder brothers were in college, my younger brother in school and my youngest sister still a child. Till then, all our studies and lives had depended on our father's income. But with his death, that income died.

Courage, Compassion and Confidence

I remember all of us standing around my mother on hearing of our father's death, devastated, wondering what she would do next. If she had confined herself to her grief, crying all the time, our lives would have been finished. Our family was bereft of the sole breadwinner and the future looked bleak. Instead, we saw her rising to the occasion, saw her new boldness, self-confidence, courage, administrative skill and her presence of mind blossoming, as she determinedly fought life's turmoil and won.

She employed labourers and began farming our lands, working strenuously. And as we looked at her, we realized a truth, that all of us had the ability to work hard. Seeing her working tirelessly, we concluded that we too should never be idle in any circumstances.

My mother handled those critical moments deftly and never showed us her fear. All we saw was her mental strength. All we learnt was that she could face anything and that she was never weighed down by negative thoughts. Her favourite words, when faced with any predicament, were: 'It is possible; it will happen; chances are bright... ' And with those words, she made everything possible!

I remember her telling me, 'Only those people who are full of love, respect and kindness are those of high status!' I saw that love; I saw her showing the same love to her relatives and to her labourers. Never once did she tell others about the difficulties she was facing. She always lent a helping hand—financially and otherwise—to anyone who came to her with a difficulty. And despite all this, she had a dream and a goal for each one of us and led us towards that target. Today, the reason each of us has reached great heights is all thanks to our dear mother. She believed in herself, shouldered her responsibilities and helped us realize our dreams.

Here's what I learned and what you can learn too: that you have to believe in yourself.

Self-belief

Yes, it's as simple as that. Believe in yourself because finally, it's only you who can do the miracle in your life. Just walk over to a mirror and look at yourself. What do you see? A broad forehead, measured gaze, a very definite nose, fine teeth, small ears and, I'm sure, a sharp brain to think and let's not forget, your two hands to work with. Now, think for a moment. What power is this that has wonderfully calculated all the proportions of your face and body and formed them in such a way that they can do so many things? These thoughts resulted in my belief in God. Yes, an intellectual quest led me to my spiritual belief, which also made me realize did that whatever work I did had to be done as perfectly as the creator who'd created me. Next came the thought that I needed to be fearful enough to know that there is someone who watches the path I tread. So, God came into my life as a higher power. I am not talking of any particular religion here, but rather of His image in the form of humanity, compassion and kindness. I believe that we first need to believe in ourselves and that automatically our belief in God follows.

My self-belief also gave me a form of self-assurance: It helped me to become dynamic and active and also helped me enjoy the habit of looking smart, of wearing clean and ironed clothes. I still remember many people in the village who admired me while I was on my way to school in the mornings, impressed by my smart-looking, tucked-in shirt. I also invested in myself by developing an interest in education and sports and cultivated the habit of reading books. Apart from my usual lessons, I avidly read books related to society, general knowledge and the biographies of leaders. Another habit that I inculcated was to maintain a close rapport with relatives and friends. I also liked helping those who were not as well off as I was. How did that happen? Well, I used to watch my parents feel happy as they helped those who had no means and I picked up this quality from them.

My schooling shaped my character during the influential years. I do believe that a teacher has the capacity to shape the future of their students. Some of my teachers, like Mr K. Jeyabalan, encouraged me to question and clarified my doubts. Treating students with equality was another striking quality which impressed me in school. After finishing school, I began college life, which meant cycling thirty-two kilometres a day to Aditanar College in Tiruchendur.

As I spent time in school and college, I learnt another important lesson in my journey of self-belief—that working towards the development of people around you creates a better future for you and the society you live in.

These were my initial lessons as I learnt to believe in myself.

There's much to learn from what we've just read. A large part of our self-confidence can come from dressing well and adopting a self-assured body language. Even as a child, I dressed well, which impressed both my friends and neighbours. My self-assurance came from the knowledge that I gathered from reading a variety of books. This also motivated me to dream big.

My desire to scale great heights inspired me to study a newly introduced course—Bachelor of Business Administration (BBA)—in a college far from home. The arduous thirty-two kilometres of daily travel did not deter me; it was a course that had a goal. And, from that course, very different from the mainstream at that time, came my ability to be successful in my business ventures later.

In this chapter, we also see the need for the right icons, heroes and gurus in life. I was awed by the way Canon Margoschis made a huge difference to Nazareth. I was motivated to do the same, especially to help make women's lives better by removing or lessening the drudgery of their time in the kitchen.

Also, like Canon Margoschis, I decided to change what I could and where I could. This reminds me of the writer who had a habit of walking on the beach every morning before he began his work. One morning after a big storm had passed, he found the whole beach littered with starfish as far as the eye could see, stretching in all directions. In the distance, he noticed a small boy continuously bending down to pick something up and throwing it into the sea.

'May I ask what it is that you are doing?' asked the writer.

The young boy paused, looked up, and replied, 'Throwing the starfish back into the ocean. When the sun rises higher they will die, unless I throw them back into the water.'

The man replied, 'But there must be tens of thousands of starfish on the beach. I'm afraid you won't really be able to make much of a difference.'

The boy bent down, picked up yet another starfish and threw

it as far as he could into the ocean. Then he turned, smiled and said, 'It made a difference to that one!'[1]

Just like the little boy made a difference to the starfish he threw back into the sea, I started making a difference in the lives of people who resided near my factories. Knowing that the men did not support their families monetarily, I offered employment to the women to help them become financially independent. The women were not only offered employment, but also trained and placed in jobs that matched their skill sets. I always knew that a woman could run a family with admirably high standards. I found that an employed woman not only managed her family but also saved money to educate her children. Thus, like the boy throwing starfish into the sea, I was able to bring about a change in society in a slow but sure and steady manner.

In this chapter, we also learn how our character can be influenced by family and upbringing. The values that I imbibed during my formative years were derived from my parents and teachers. I got inspiration from my beloved mother, who still continues to motivate me as a role model, even after her demise. The values that I imbibed from her, have stood me in good stead and helped me overcome the hurdles I faced time and again in business. Through my highs and lows, the learning from my childhood helped me handle both failures and success equally.

Now look around you for lessons that will help you start believing in yourself. Your town or your village has a history and people from whom you can learn great lessons. Start moving away from the selfish thought of just helping yourself; remember that all the help that you offer others returns to you. Remember that adversity brings out the

---

[1] Adapted from *The Star Thrower* by Loren Eiseley (1907–77).

best in you and that death, financial setbacks, poverty are all good starting points. Compassion and love for others are not weaknesses but things that strengthen an individual and build a strong leader. And, last but not the least, hard work pays like nothing else does!

2

THINKING BEYOND THE ORDINARY

I believed in dreaming big about the future.

Our beloved former President Dr A.P.J. Abdul Kalam said, 'Dreams are not what you see while asleep. Dreams are what won't let you sleep.' These dreams shake you out of your comfort zone and help you build a good future. I'm sure many may not like the idea of 'moving out of your comfort zone'. Choosing a course in business studies to help achieve my goal, disrupted my routine and the comfortable life I led in Nazareth. I could easily have chosen the arts or science courses like most others did, available in the local college, but instead I chose to go the extra mile, literally, by travelling back and forth to Tiruchendur, 32 kilometres away, to attend college.

Education, beyond the Ordinary

In those days, it was expected that one would graduate with a degree in the arts or science and automatically become a teacher. There were plenty of employment opportunities in the higher education sector, thanks to the focused efforts of the missionaries who came to spread education. Following my example, my siblings too opted for a career that had nothing to do with agriculture, which had been the family business till that time. Our head of the department, Dr Joseph Rayappan, was our source of inspiration. Even while explaining that the course was a relatively new one, he insisted that we maintain a formal dress code of a neatly pressed shirt, formal trousers, polished shoes and a necktie. This practice immediately gave us immense confidence and courage, when compared to the other informally dressed students. This discipline also added a touch of seriousness to the course and we could already see ourselves as entrepreneurs and business professionals in the making. Even today, I ensure that I am well-groomed every day and encourage my children and employees to follow suit.

However, dreaming is not enough! Dreams need to be followed by action. My dream was to start a business of my own. My grandfather and father inspired me and passed on their entrepreneurial skills to me. I was also inspired by my uncle, my father's cousin, who had a public transport business in my hometown. I had seen him managing the business on a day-to-day basis, since my childhood. And, since we all lived in a joint family, I could closely observe how he managed his business, and these insights kindled my interest all the more.

Unconventional Thinking in a Conventional Job

I worked as a medical representative in my first job and it made me realize that I was a people person and loved to interact with different customers like chemists, druggists and doctors on a constant basis. My next job at Godrej Soaps Ltd as a sales representative was a challenging but interesting one. I picked up the art of selling in the vast arena of the marketplace, where I had to interact with distributors and retailers of all kinds. These retailers were an unorganized lot those days, unlike today's market that includes a sizeable modern segment of retailers. This job gave me a huge opportunity not only to interact with people, but also to study the market preferences and spending pattern of consumers, especially women, at close quarters.

My role in this fast-moving consumer goods (FMCG) company was to control and manage retailers in my designated territory, ably supported by distributors. A few revenue districts also came within my sales territory. The role of a company representative was to appoint distributors in identified areas within his assigned territory and then to effect primary sales by helping them to redistribute stocks/products in impressive quantities using promotional schemes. My strength lay in my keen observation of the distribution pattern of my company and that helped me get a feel of it first, before attempting to try my hand at strategizing promotional schemes for implementation. While rolling out plans, I would absorb trade secrets shared with me by the company and then go about devising better ones. I generally made a habit of sharing my plans with the workers under my supervision and encouraged them to suggest improvements. After that, I worked hard to achieve the goal that had been set.

During this time, I realized that there was ample scope to experiment with innovative ideas to achieve the targets set by the company. In those days, the company helped in the redistribution process by introducing schemes that would make retailers stock more of their products. These incentive schemes made small retailers make purchases in larger quantities, as the company gave a percentage of the profits to them for buying more. A small retailer who normally bought six pieces of an item like toilet soap felt encouraged to buy more and landed up, quite often, purchasing a dozen!

For example, if an 8 per cent incentive was offered on a product like soap, the redistribution plan chalked out by the company representative would allow retailers to have one soap free, for a dozen purchased. Product targets were fixed and such schemes were used to push products into the retail market to achieve those same targets. Such practices continue in the distribution set-up of FMCGs in the Indian marketplace till today.

However, while the other officers in my company offered straight schemes of free soaps as quantity purchase schemes (QPS), I decided to think out of the box and look beyond the ordinary. I'd found several retail outlets manned by women, who were either the wives or family members of the retailers. These women would run the shops when their husbands or family members went to the market to buy goods. During these times, I had the chance to interact with these women on a personal basis, and get to understand them, thereby getting to know their needs. Based on this, I modified our company schemes to satisfy their needs and created offers to attract their interest. For example, I offered them a stainless steel plate free, on the purchase of a dozen soaps and the women jumped at it, as these articles were very useful. During summer, a table fan or a ceiling fan was offered to them. Such schemes were an instant hit and the volume of purchases scaled up remarkably. In the process, I managed to win a special place in the minds of the retail ecosystem.

I cashed in on the influential power of my women customers to escalate sales, as I was able to convince the wives of the shopkeepers to induce purchases in higher quantities. Soon, the freebies on quantity purchase came to be planned after looking at their future requirements, based on brainstorming with them. Gradually, the distributor's support stepped up, and he was able to get the backing of not only the retailer, but also his family. This helped me to surpass my targets easily and create new records. My general manager, A.K.S. Rao appreciated my efforts and cited my success as an example to the other sales people, and would often ask me to share these tales of success with them during sales meetings. Such innovative ideas, coupled with my ability to manage my territory efficiently, earned me promotions much earlier than many other senior colleagues.

Using Innovation to Sell a Difficult Product

When Godrej launched their powder hair dye for the first time, I was given the task of selling them in Tirunelveli district, which I was in charge of.

I was saddened to see that the same market that had once sold my earlier products in large quantities, refused even to give me an ear now. As this was the response of small retailers, there was no doubt that it would be the same with the bigger retailers. I was very upset that my efforts were not bearing fruit, but still did not lose hope, realizing that I could still rely on my innovative thinking. One day, I came across a roadside market where cows were being sold. I paused for a while and observed that the white cows were fetching higher prices than the others. I imagined how attractive a white cow would look with a black tail, and how its price could soar!

As many people know, buyers estimate the age of a cow by the colour of the tail and the condition of the teeth. The darker the tail, the younger the cow is deemed to be. So, cows with darker tails fetched higher prices in the market. An idea struck me and I immediately applied the powder hair dye on the tail of a cow. Then, I stood back to watch the response, along with the owner of the cow. I was pleased to note that the cow was sold earlier than those with a natural white tail. This news spread fast among the cow-sellers and I was asked to wave my magic wand by applying Godrej powder hair dye on a few more cows. The cow-sellers now wanted to buy the product, and I realized that I had created a new market for a hair dye, in a completely different way!

Again, I proved that out-of-the-box thinking paid rich dividends. I learnt many things from my experience at Godrej and they laid the foundation for my masala business later on. A.K.S. Rao constantly motivated me to do new things in different ways and highlighted my successes. These innovative ideas became the model for scheme operations in the company, and all other territories were told to operate such schemes to augment their sales. Mr Rao often asked me to pitch my ideas during sales meetings, to help improvise on schemes designed by the company, for an easier acceptance by retailers. I rose in my chosen career because I dared to think beyond the ordinary!

I always thought differently. I had the innate ability to initiate innovative promotions.

Do you remember a popular video called 'Lead India', that went viral recently? It showed leadership qualities through the heroics of a little boy. The video begins with a road blocked by a fallen tree after heavy rain. Traffic piles up and pedestrians, cyclists and motorists all wonder when the road will be cleared, so that they can continue on their respective journeys. A little distance away, a group of young boys are happily playing in the rainwater, jumping and splashing, enjoying themselves. Slowly, they become aware of the traffic jam and wonder why nobody is taking the initiative to clear the mess, instead of honking. One little boy stops playing, moves to the fallen tree, and tries to move it with his tender hands, all by himself. There is a hush and suddenly, from all round, cyclists, motorists and others come to his rescue to push the tree aside, and traffic moves again. All it took was the effort of one little fellow who was not happy just playing, but wanted to make a difference. The qualities which I exhibited when I used to devise promotional schemes, by trying out what others never thought of, may be equated to the efforts made by the little boy to restore normalcy.

There is another little fable that bears some similarity to what I did: We have all heard the story of the hare and the lion, which reveals how critical and different thinking helped a hare save his own life and those of his compatriots. As the story goes, all the animals were scared of the lion, the king of the jungle, as he preyed on them to satisfy his hunger. They were always worried for their lives, so they held a meeting, hoping to devise a plan to save themselves. An old wise hare stood up and suggested that they send one of their own, voluntarily, to the lion each day, instead of being attacked by the lion. All the animals agreed to this plan and they went to the lion. The wise hare explained their idea to the lion, who readily agreed.

The day of the hare's turn arrived, but he was determined to live, so he hatched a plan to save himself. So, he reached the lion late. The hungry lion was walking up and down angrily, and asked the hare why he was late. The hare said that another lion had waylaid him and told him that he was stronger than this lion and so should be treated as the king of the jungle. Hearing this, the hungry lion became angrier and asked the hare to take him to the other lion.

The hare led him to a deep well and told the lion that the other beast was inside. The angry lion looked into the well, saw his own image in the water and mistook it for another lion. Furious, he jumped into the well to kill the other lion and died himself. All the other animals were relieved. Their lives were saved by the clever thinking of the old hare and they appreciated his wisdom and lived happily after that.

This story not only reflects that wisdom is stronger than strength, but also that it is out-of-the-box thinking that the hare used to save not only his life but also the lives of the other animals who lived with him in the jungle.

Just like the hare, I also did a lot of strategic and analytical thinking, which proved, not only to A.K.S. Rao, but also to my peers and superiors, that moving out of their comfort zones and working with passion can help everyone easily achieve their goals. The risks I took to develop innovative promotional schemes saw immediate phenomenal results and, with the active involvement of my teammates, I was able to surpass the targets set by the company.

Thinking beyond the ordinary will undoubtedly help you, whether you are an executive, an entrepreneur or even someone who is just venturing out to become successful in your chosen path. Remember to follow your dreams with action. Develop the habit of keen observation, in order to stay abreast of the latest changes. Also, keep in mind that a setback is the first step to success and will only increase your determination to reach your goal. Most importantly, learn to take risks through alternative and out-of-the-box thinking, even while you are passionate about going beyond your comfort zone. Last, but not the least, be a team person because working collectively brings results in multiples!

3

INTRAPRENEURSHIP: THE MANAGEMENT PHILOSOPHY OF SUCCESS

I decided to do things differently!

While working for Godrej, my passion for the execution of my responsibilities knew no bounds. I would do everything sincerely and leave no stone unturned until I had accomplished the goals that we, as a team, set for ourselves. I was aware that the normal way of working yielded just about average results, so, I decided to do things differently, because I had the ability to think and act differently.

How Intrapreneurship Became an Integral Part of My Life

Every employee was given key result areas and targets and was expected to fulfil the same. Most of the people in the company, in those days, followed a stereotypical way of working. However, I thought differently and, very often, asked myself this question, 'If the company was my own and I worked for myself, how would I work?' Different answers came to my mind: 'I would not look at the watch and work! I would complete the job on time! I would not waste the money allocated by the company for standard product promotions and would instead think up schemes that yield sure results...' All these answers pointed to one single concept: of working like an owner and entrepreneur within my field of work. And, thus, I discovered 'intrapreneurship', to take ownership of what you do even when you work for an organization and achieve otherwise unattainable results!

Whenever Godrej introduced new products, we opened 'Special Counters' at important locations all over the city. People were enticed through video clippings or audio publicity to come to these counters. There, they would be told what the products were all about, how they were special—whether in quality, cost etc.—and comparative valuations against the products of other companies would be shown to them. I decided to work round-the-clock whenever such counters were opened.

During the early days of my marriage, the company introduced a new washing soap and a special counter was opened at an important place in the city.

When I got ready to go to work in the morning, I asked my wife Thelma whether she was willing to come with me. She hesitated, wondering what she would do there, but I persuaded her, saying that she would enjoy seeing other people, instead of sitting all alone at home.

She accompanied me to the counter and began to observe what was happening. Since it was a reputed company and the product was given a lot of publicity, a large number of people crowded the counter. They wanted to know all the details about the soap and I answered every query patiently. Thelma, meanwhile, was observing how I welcomed customers and patiently handled them, explaining everything to them clearly and calmly. That day, she learnt that there were different types of customers and when questions were asked about a new product, how important it was to answer them patiently.

Intrapreneurship and Demanding Customers

Thelma gently asked me on our way home, 'When many of the women asked tricky questions about that product, how is it that I didn't ever see you get angry?'

My reply was, 'Thelma, Gandhiji had said that customers are like God. Though we may not think of them as God, we should consider them with respect and not be annoyed. This thought helps me to explain things well to them. I consider all my customers to be my friends and I respect women!' I saw Thelma nod and I continued, 'So, I never get angry when they ask me any questions. Of course, many test my patience but, instead of losing my temper, I tell myself that God has sent them to me as training to reduce my anger. Anger is what we use on our enemies, but if we use the weapon of anger against everyone, it would boomerang and come back to us! When we are angry, we lose our calm, ruin our health and age faster. So, Thelma, I believe that to remain healthy and positive we need to control our anger.' As Thelma smiled in agreement, I said, 'Also, remember, my company pays me well and it is my responsibility to satisfy my customers!'

Believing in the Product

On reaching home, I hurried to the bathroom with the newly-introduced soap bar, carrying one coloured and one white shirt with me. Thelma wondered why I was doing so, when it was she who had been washing my clothes all along. She told me to stop doing the washing and go to bed.

I told her, 'I have made all my customers believe that the soap is excellent. Tomorrow, I will be saying the same; before doing that, I need to know the nature of this soap. Only then will I sleep peacefully. Let me use it and find out its quality.' I proceeded to wash the two shirts and hung them up to dry.

I had also given this soap to everyone who worked with me, telling them to use it that night. I intended to ask them their opinion the next morning. If their response happened to be negative, I had decided to take it up with my higher authorities.

When you create your own product, you first test it to see how good it is and then you reassure your customers that they are buying the best. I did the same thing and worked like an entrepreneur myself. That is the very essence of intrapreneurship.

As an intrapreneur, you treat the customers of your company's products as if they were your own, with patience and respect. In other words, you have integrated yourself into the company and with its products and this ownership not only yields sure results but it also makes you feel like a brand ambassador.

While reading about the success story of Dhirubhai Ambani, I came to know that he used to have a job in Aden, with a large transcontinental commodities trading firm, A. Besse & Co. Later, he was transferred to the section that dealt with petroleum products for the oil firm, Shell. While he quickly learnt the tricks of the trade, Mr Ambani said that he worked with great involvement to learn from everything that was assigned to him, in order to excel in what he did. He worked hard with his willpower and attitude, aligned completely like the owner of the business, and finally learned the ropes of the business. When he returned to India and started his own business, he said that he did not have to change his working style, as he had already practised working like an 'owner' in Aden. His success is now part of the annals of business history. His story shows us exemplary evidence of how success is the fruit of the management philosophy of intrapreneurship.

In this chapter, we can clearly see my wholehearted involvement in both my company and its products. My passion for my job was evident in my patient handling of difficult customers, as well as in the thorough knowledge of my products, which helped me answer questions confidently. From this, we realize the importance of adopting a thorough customer-centric approach. Besides this, the respect I showed to all my customers, especially women, helped me to increase my company's sales. The ability to observe different reactions to the product also helped me develop newer and novel methods to convert customer curiosity into a definite purchase decision.

When I tested the soaps personally, it showed that I needed to be personally convinced about my product, before selling it successfully with total conviction. Quite often, my clothesline at home would bear an array of square pieces of cloth—both white and coloured—and visitors were struck by this proof of my intense passion for my job. I do not differentiate myself from my employer and adopt necessary measures to ensure customer satisfaction. These actions of mine, in which I expected nothing in return, form the basis of 'intrapreneurship'.

I realized that small retailers have a large potential to excel in India, even though large manufacturers do not pay any special attention to them. I worked on innovative methods to not only push a product, but also to instil confidence in the minds of these retailers to bring out their latent talents, so that they could emerge as intrapreneurs. The novel promotional schemes

I conceptualized and implemented in the marketplace, stood me in good stead and played a significant role in helping me gain acceptance among my retailer friends. By propagating the spirit of 'each owning what each one does' among retail workers, I was churning out successful intrapreneurs on a sustainable basis.

When we read the success story of Dhirubhai Ambani, we are able to trace a degree of commonality between us. It commences from having a small start, being totally involved in whatever work we undertook, and taking ownership of our responsibilities in both spirit and deed.

Here are some of the tenets of intrapreneurship that we can derive for ourselves.

Intrapreneurship is total dedication: Those following the concept of intrapreneurship in their workplaces are totally involved in their jobs. They will not stray from their focus until they achieve their objectives. Even if they have to spend sleepless nights to achieve the desired results, they do so quite willingly and happily, with utter dedication.

Intrapreneurship is unsupervised leadership: Intrapreneurs do not need any supervision. They do not work for their bosses. Rather, they work for the fulfilment of objectives, as if they are working for themselves and not for anyone else. They have a latent leadership quality, which surfaces as they become more and more passionate about their job, and find ways and means of doing things effectively and fruitfully.

Intrapreneurship means having a never-give-up attitude: The innate strength of intrapreneurs is never to give up on anything they undertake and to complete the job. Even if there are hurdles and setbacks, intrapreneurs should consider them to be temporary and should strive zealously to get results in the end, forging ahead with a never-give-up attitude.

Intrapreneurship is innovative execution: One of the most significant principles of intrapreneurship is innovative thinking, in order to arrive at newer methods of job execution. Intrapreneurs always think out of the box and never hesitate to find better ways to achieve their targets.

> *Learning from the above, we should ask ourselves, 'If this was my company, would I work any differently from how I am working now? Do I take ownership of whatever I do? Will I test a product myself first, to convince myself of the quality of what my company produces and sells or what I may produce and sell?'*

> *We have to learn that innovative thinking alone is not enough and it needs the support of innovative execution. And finally, we must realize that intrapreneurship is all about paving the way to our own success.*

4

LEARNING TO TIDE OVER DIFFICULTIES

Let's overcome difficulties!

Heavy rains are a problem indeed. But, once the rainwater washes all the debris away, rivers become clean. Similarly, big problems arrive without an announcement, attack us suddenly and try to shake us up. But, when we stand unmoved, we realize that they have taught us a great lesson about our resilience. We don't have to be anxious when we face problems; all we have to do is to be strong like a mountain! Those who go through numerous difficulties become experienced in handling them and, in the process, they learn to be patient.

I believe that there are two ways to prevent difficulties from overcoming us.

The first one is to be content with what we have. This is like watching the sea from the shore, without wetting our legs.

The second one is to create self-confidence, so that we can achieve whatever we decide to. This is like getting into a boat to go fishing, despite there being giant waves.

I believe in the second way. I move ahead with confidence. I know that I have to take the first step in order to reach the goal.

Build Self-confidence in Simple Ways

I have been dynamic and active since childhood. Since then, looking good and being presentable was my first step in confidence-building and it continued throughout my life. Being well-groomed gave me the confidence to face people. Thereafter, I realized that if I was well-prepared beforehand, I would be confident. Whenever I prepared myself in advance by going through the subjects that would be taught, I went to my classes with confidence. Being well-prepared, whether in academics or in any other task, is what gives us confidence. I was also an avid reader, apart from my regular subjects of study. I read books about society, general knowledge, biographies and so on.

Also, it is no secret that a good physique gives confidence. From childhood, I had taken a great interest in education, as well as in sports. I must say that the people of Nazareth have always been robust in physical health. As students, we vied with each other to score well in academics. After class, we used to rush to the playground to play football, a game the dwellers of Nazareth loved.

When we look neat and presentable, prepare beforehand and keep ourselves fit and healthy, we develop the confidence to face people and the strength to handle any situation.

Take the First Step and Family Support Follows

Till the end of my school years, I hardly felt any hardships in life. My life revolved around studying and sports and my father took every care of the family. After the death of my father, everything turned topsy-turvy and our family became financially weak.

As recounted earlier, after successfully finishing high school, I decided to join Aditanar College in Tiruchendur. This wonderful college, founded by C.P. Aditanar, the founder of We Tamils, a political party, was sixteen kilometres away from Nazareth. I had always wanted to study there, but since we were not very well off, I did not express this desire to my mother. She was already stretched financially in raising all of us with the little money she got from rearing cattle and hens. I was quite aware of her hardships, though she never showed any signs of struggle. It was not easy for her to provide food, clothing and education to all of us. Since it was my mother's principle to not borrow money from anyone, she invested her life in hard work.

I realized that to join Aditanar College, a lot of money would be needed and my mother would have to work harder. She used to get up very early in the morning to begin her strenuous work. If I joined college, she would have to get up even earlier and go to bed later, thereby affecting her health.

But, somehow, my mother came to know of my desires, around the same time that my brother was studying in a college in Srivaikundam.

One night, when I returned home from my game of football, my mother approached me fondly and said, 'People may say that we are struggling, but we have no difficulties. We eat well, wear good clothes and never borrow, unlike some of the people here who borrow often.' Immediately, I realized that my mother had understood my wishes.

The mother was the fairy that always granted my wishes. She asked me, 'Your elder brother is in Srivaikundam College, which college do you want to join?' Without waiting for my answer, she unfolded the end of her sari and showed me wads of money, which she had saved with great difficulty. My eyes became moist on seeing this. Every rupee was the result of my mother's sweat, saved through years of untiring work, day and night. Even when I had been in school, she had been saving for my college. I understood what she was trying to say and told her that I would like to study at Aditanar College.

In those days, there was a passenger train that plied between Nazareth and Tiruchendur every morning. It was my idea to go by that train to college and avail of a monthly concessional pass for students.

Be a Hands-on Person

My mother was hands-on in everything she did. She would do everything herself first, so that she had a complete understanding of how it was done. I was amazed by her administrative capacity. She was extremely good at helping the family develop, through good planning and personal administration. She used to buy cattle after evaluating their worth. She visited the market, understood the price and value for everything, ranging from consumables to cattle. She was even able to make the right estimate of the milk given by each cow, through her experience. As I'd mentioned earlier, she would get up early in the morning to milk the cows. She would sell the sheep and take good care of the hens, through which she earned money. Shopkeepers conducted their business from commercial premises, but my mother did an even better job while staying at home and rearing these cattle and hens. I've often told her that her 'business blood' runs in me, which is what has made me a successful businessman. When I expressed my desire to study business administration and learn business management, she hugged me tight and kissed me. As she did so, I felt that I'd already become a businessman. I felt ecstatic!

Where There's a Will, There's a Way

When I was in the sixth standard at Margoschis School, K. Jeyabalan was my class teacher. He is currently eighty-three years old and has thirty-five years of teaching experience. Even today, he remembers me standing before him, a boy in short pants! He shared his remembrance of me as a student and said, 'Though I was the class teacher for Padmasingh Isaac when he was in the sixth standard, he studied under me till his Secondary School Leaving Certificate (SSLC, the then eleventh standard) examinations. I was a science teacher and my teaching method was always different from the others. When the school reopened in June, I used to get six new sticks, which by the end of each academic year would be broken. I had realized from experience that students would learn with full concentration only if they were punished. If they had scored low marks, I would make them stand on the bench and give impositions from the relevant subjects to coach them. No student had ever escaped my punishment.

'Students who had a great interest in learning and never criticized me learnt well, out of fear. In my experience, not one parent had ever asked me why I had punished their son. In those days, parents believed that teachers punished students with good reason and that these students would improve in life.

'Even Isaac might have got beatings from me. But I don't remember those occasions much. At the same time, I remember him as a neatly dressed lad, asking many questions in my classes. Many a time, I had appreciated him for his interest in learning. Today, I am so happy to say that I was his teacher.'

After my SSLC examination, I joined Aditanar College and travelled by train, but unfortunately the railway service was stopped and then my mother bought me a bicycle. Every day, I bicycled thirty-two kilometres to college and back home, sometimes weathering heavy rain and, most often, a scorching sun. Sometimes, when the tyres of the bicycle got punctured, I ended up pushing it. At college, I studied with great difficulty but with immense interest. I faced difficulties and challenges with my inborn confidence. While the absence of the train service posed a challenge, I overcame it by bicycling and eventually came to enjoy the experience. Had I considered it a difficult task, tiredness would have undoubtedly played spoilsport!

More than the college syllabus, I was keen on reading reference books on business management which were available in the library. Finally, I completed my studies, emerging as the best student in the college.

From 1968 to 1998, Professor Ladislaus Rodrigo of Veerapandianpatnam near Nazareth taught industrial psychology at Aditanar College. Today, he is eighty-two years old. He shared his thoughts on me in an interview. 'Memories of Padmasingh Isaac are still fresh in my mind. Isaac was my student. I met him thirty years later, after he had become a brilliant businessman. Since I had taught quite a number of students, I don't remember everyone's face but when I met Padmasingh Isaac after he became a businessman in Chennai, I could identify him as my student, despite having had no connection with him for the past thirty years.

'I noticed his keen sense of observation and his ability to evaluate. He also behaved like a gentleman. More than a good businessman, he is a good man. Teachers do play a role in a student's success. I don't remember what lessons I taught him. But he has learnt well and picked up all that he had to learn, both from the college and from society. That's why he has reached this level of success and has become a textbook himself for the whole student community.'

Today, I'm happy that my life has turned out to be a good textbook for the younger generations. I developed two strong qualities as a result of the difficulties I faced.

The first of these is self-confidence. The success of a learner does not come from academic studies alone, but is a result of a 'I can do it' attitude that only comes from self-confidence. Often, the only deterrent to a positive attitude is a feeling of shame, springing from a sense of unworthiness. It prevents us from being confident, makes us fear failure and stops us from attempting things, thinking that they are not 'dignified' jobs!

I can say emphatically that we should throw away the feeling of shame that clouds our mind. Shame cannot accompany us on our journey towards success.

Mahatma Gandhi (whom I admire greatly for his courage and self-confidence) is the best example of someone who emerged victorious against shameful circumstances. In South Africa, he faced racial discrimination and was not allowed to travel in the first class and he was even thrown off a train at Pietermaritzburg. He was also beaten up by a driver of a stagecoach for refusing to make room for a European passenger. He was denied entry to several hotels. On one occasion, the magistrate of a court in Durban ordered Gandhiji to remove his turban and on another, he was kicked by a police officer off a footpath, which was out of bounds for Indians in South Africa. If shame had deterred him, Mahatma Gandhi would not have been able to achieve what he did in his lifetime for his country and countrymen.

The second quality is perseverance. My mother, Flora Isaac, is the epitome of perseverance. She single-handedly raised her children by working all day. She sacrificed her entire life for them. She planned her resources to save enough for the education of her children. Despite difficulties, my mother left no stone unturned to shape the future of her children. Her way of life impacted my life greatly and I learnt the most important principle from her, that of tireless perseverance. I imbibed this lesson of perseverance from my mother and applied it to my successful business later.

Remember to focus on what you do and remember that challenges can be overcome only if you throw yourself into them—no pain, no gain. Remember that self-confidence opens the door to success and that perseverance paves the way to your goal. Also, remember to express yourself clearly and simply. And, last but not least, feeling hesitant or unsure can only be an impediment in your journey towards success!

5

MOVING OUT OF YOUR COMFORT ZONE MEANS WELCOMING NEW OPPORTUNITIES

Change is the only constant.

Changes are inevitable in life and occur every day. We should try to adapt ourselves to them and only then will we be able to move on and progress, otherwise our lives will come to a halt. It is the rust that destroys iron. Likewise, it is anger and frustration that destroy us. But, when you move out of your comfort zone, then, like a cloud that moves to reveal the moon behind it, you enjoy peace!

Moving Out of Our Comfort Zone

When my father was alive, he got my sister Saroja married to a central government employee, Paul Devaraj, who was in Chennai. So after the marriage, Saroja settled there with her husband. One by one, all my siblings went to Chennai and in a way my brother-in-law was the reason behind this. They firmly believed that they could reach great heights of success only if they moved to a big city. After finishing college, both my elder brothers Rajasingh and Augustine Isaac also left for Chennai. Augustine first worked for a while in the shop run by our uncle, and later, he started his own grocery shop named Mala Store in Purasawalkam. The business flourished. Meanwhile, Rajasingh became a higher secondary school teacher in the city. Both of them got married and settled there, in the city of opportunities.

After completing my BBA successfully, I was faced with the dilemma of whether to look for job opportunities in and around my town or to go to Chennai. Nazareth and its surroundings were my comfort zones, with all my friends and classmates living in the neighbouring towns. But, I was prepared to go to Chennai to look for jobs. I knew that going there was not going to be a bed of roses and opportunities would not just fall into my lap. I went to Chennai and stayed with my brothers. I prepared myself, since I knew my weaknesses. Though I was well-groomed, I realized that I had to improve my communication skills. I could understand what people said, but had some difficulty in replying in English. I started working on this by reading English newspapers regularly. Then I started talking in English to friends in the neighbourhood. An Anglo-Indian teacher in Purasawalkam helped me improve, and soon I could speak English well. The job interviews were in English but I managed to answer questions well and soon got a job in the reputed Godrej company. I first became a sales representative, responsible for managing the company's sales in the Tirunelveli branch, and had to visit Chennai for official purposes.

Uprooting Oneself Isn't Easy

Meanwhile, I used to give a major portion of my earnings to my mother in Nazareth. Soon, my younger brother Topsingh too came to Chennai and established a shop called Sahayam Traders in Purasawalkam.

All of us were now in Chennai, leaving my mother back in Nazareth. She often felt quite lonely and only had my youngest sister Baby with her. She, who had toiled hard for the welfare of her children, longed to have them around her always. She nurtured the desire to tend a cheerful home for us. Earlier, when she used to cook for us, she also enjoyed watching us relishing the food. Now, she was denied this happiness. She could not handle the separation and stopped eating properly.

This caused much concern among us in Chennai. I wanted to bring her back to her old self and went back to Nazareth to speak to her.

'Mother,' I said, 'we need to change according to the situation and business opportunities. Only then can our conditions improve. Look around you, so many people from Nazareth have gone abroad for jobs and brought prosperity to this village. Even Dad went overseas to Colombo. You, too, practised farming and cattle-rearing and brought us up. Likewise, to do well, we have to settle in Chennai, which has plenty of commercial and business opportunities. Don't worry about us. Now that we have started working, there is no need for you to work any more.'

She looked at me and smiled, and I continued, 'But we need your guidance. With your advice, we can prosper. So, we need you in Chennai to help us. Soon, I will receive my promotion and will also be transferred to Chennai, so please come and be with us!' She did not accept my request immediately. She'd been in Nazareth all her life and did not have the heart to leave the town or its people. But I persisted and got her to change her mind. She finally decided to move out of her comfort zone and come to Chennai, handing over the responsibilities of the land to a relative. In Chennai, she lived with my brother Augustine Isaac's family.

After the Pain Comes the Gains

My mother's arrival in Chennai was a big relief for me and after this I was able to devote all my time to grow in my company and move to the next level. I toiled hard. Our products were mostly sold in the southern districts of Tamil Nadu. I had been successful in selling them to retailers using detailed planning, but did not stop with just doing that as the sales manager; rather, I began to observe the work and attitude of small-scale businessmen and to admire their honesty, hard work and dedication. Many small retailers who had set up shop in and around Chennai were from the district of Tirunelveli and they were born businessmen. They knew how to buy intelligently and sell prudently. As part of my routine, I visited more than a hundred such small shops every day to get orders, and began to observe the services they extended to their customers, which came genuinely and truly from their hearts. They completely devoted themselves to their business and to their customers. Their contribution to society was unparalleled. They were the ones who actually brought the warmth of the villages into the cities when they moved there to improve their own lives. I salute them from the bottom of my heart!

Many aspects of their contribution often went unnoticed. When people buy land in the outskirts of a city, they automatically search for small shops in that area. They determine the prospects of that area by enquiring with the shopkeepers, who are knowledgeable about their surroundings. Here, the small retailer helps to determine the value of the land.

To get any counsel, to admit a child to school or to take someone to a local doctor or to get some money urgently, one goes to a small shop nearby even today. The small retailer, who is experienced and has all the news of the neighbourhood, acts as an advisor and guide.

When essentials need to be bought immediately, people cannot travel long distances. The shopkeeper goes to the city market every day and helps his customers by procuring these essentials. With this service, the shop acts as an excellent service centre.

A small retailer also has information about people living in the area, how they are related to one another and about their special days and celebrations. When necessary, he shares this information with others. Here, the shopkeeper is like an excellent public relations officer.

It is small-scale businessmen who get up early in the morning and buy the things needed by people—vegetables, fruits and groceries—and sell them at a reasonable price, thereby playing the role of a helper catering to the needs of customers.

Often, the little shop is a stepping stone to the first job. A parent exclaims, 'My son does not have a proper job, he idles away his time, I don't know what to do with him!' 'Don't worry,' says the shopkeeper, 'leave him in my shop. I'll teach him about life and business.' Here, the shop becomes an employment office.

Many youngsters, who were first employed in this way, eventually become shopkeepers, running their own shops. Here, these shops act as training centres to create new businessmen.

These compassionate businessmen, who are unable to see their neighbours living in want, often help them out by lending money at times of crisis and emergency. Here, the shop becomes a social bank.

In India, small retailers mean a lot, and their contribution cannot be matched by any other business. They render yeoman service to society, without seeking publicity.

My relocation to Chennai taught me many lessons, which I would not have learned otherwise. I began to gain experience in my job and also gathered the skills to analyse the success factors of small businesses. I found that small businessmen often had to sacrifice many comforts to make a significant difference and emerge successful in their business.

Let us also learn from these small-scale businessmen and move out of our comfort zones in order to succeed. Next, we need to spot potential areas that may provide great opportunities for growth and move into them immediately. Remember, like the small retailers, we must always be genuinely close to customers and finally go beyond the call of duty to satisfy them.

6

FORTUNE FAVOURS
THOSE WHO HELP THEMSELVES

Is it hard work or sheer luck that brings success?
I thought about this and realized that a lamp can give out light only when it is lit. Similarly, only those who toil are fortunate. Once, a lazy fellow who was facing many hardships was walking along a road. Seeing his plight, God pityingly dropped a pouch of gold coins before him. But the lazy man was walking so aimlessly that he did not notice the pouch. A hard-working man was behind him; this man was always aware of his surroundings and knew what was happening around him. He picked up that pouch because he was attentive. He who works hard is vigilant and he alone is able to embrace luck when it befalls him.

A Salary Shouldn't Be Your Only Goal

When I was working for Godrej in the Tirunelveli territory, my monthly salary was Rs 10,000. I did not work just for my salary, but for the experience that the job gave me in areas other than selling, such as inventory management, indenting for each distributor, sales promotion planning, managing sales events in exhibitions, managing a large sales force, conducting periodical reviews with distributors, launching new products in the market, etc. The experience I gained was phenomenal.

My company used to give me sales targets and I would willingly accept them, without considering them to be burdens. Only by accepting my work willingly could I get good results. Generally, sales people think that targets are planned by those above, and they question why they should work hard to achieve the goals that they did not plan. They think of these goals as burdens. But I always looked at my targets as personal goals and worked with all my heart, mind and spirit. I enjoyed making detailed plans to reach them. While planning, I included the trade secrets shared by the company but formulated better ones on my own. I ensured that these plans were not harsh on those who worked under me and were not difficult to implement. I would first share my plans with my team and then encourage their cooperation, while working hard with them to reach the desired targets and go beyond.

In leading by example, I set an example for other workers who learnt to work hard, like a captain motivating his soldiers. I also worked with my team of distributors and their salesmen, embracing their failures along with the successes, but maintaining a balanced objective. At the young age of twenty-five, I realized that 'a single tree can never make a grove', and that success can be attained only through teamwork. In those days, the company gave us target incentives; on achieving my target and receiving the incentive, I would share it with my fellow workers, which encouraged them to work harder.

On my visits to retail shops, I would prepare relevant

questions so as to get an idea of how to move ahead. Some of these questions were:

- What is the business like in that shop?
- Which products are sold more and why?
- Why do customers buy a particular brand?
- What is the financial position of the customers who buy from that shop?
- How much do customers spend at the shop?
- Do they buy things by cash or through credit?
- Who are the major customers, male or female?
- What age groups buy which brands?
- Do customers prefer newly introduced products?
- How are products advertised on TV evaluated by customers?
- Is there a strong emotional bond between the retailer and his customers?
- How do customers bargain?
- How do customers choose the products that they want to buy?
- How do workers in shops behave with customers?
- Are the customers who buy from that shop satisfied?
- What do the customers feel about the buying experience they've had in the shop?

Laying the Foundations for the Future

I would glean this information and write it in my diary, every day. So, you can understand what I meant when I said that a salary was not my only objective in the job; my objective was the experiences I gained, which eventually laid the foundation for my growth later.

Businesses may be made up of businessmen, but, however qualified we are in business or business techniques, it is the 'education of experience' and the 'learning of practicality', that are far more relevant than everything else. If we thoroughly learn all the lessons from our experiences and we learn to excel in our interactions with people, only then will we succeed in our business. Only when we study the human mind, can we show real love and maintain a good rapport with everyone around us, especially in the business ecosystem.

We give importance to the customer, yes, but we should also know how to give importance to the sensitivity of the human character. Study the differences between people's faces, their voices, and you will learn about different personality traits. We consider this to be a person's identity. Every person we meet in our lives, differs in their character from others. Why, even in a family the son is not like the father; or the daughter is not like the son, though they are chips off the same old block!

Man's mind is like the sea. We cannot fully understand anyone's thoughts, ideas, hopes and wishes. But when we meet many people and study them in depth, we learn to assess them to a great extent. Studying human thoughts can give us wonderful lessons. If we succeed in that, we can easily weigh a person's personality to understand them well. Through this, we develop not only the business we do but also develop deep friendships and relationships. This also helps us to excel in liaising with people.

Lessons from the World's Greats

There are lessons to be learnt from people who have achieved big business successes worldwide. Apart from analysing a person's individuality through different experiences of mine, I also avidly read about the business achievements of world-renowned businessmen and their business development. I was attracted to the story of the growth of General Electric. This company, founded by Thomas Alva Edison and a few others, holds trademarks in many fields and it is involved in several businesses, right from manufacturing the electric bulb to wind turbines for aircraft engines. The headquarters of this company are in the city of Fairfield, USA, and with three lakh employees, the company has emerged to be one of the largest conglomerates in the world.

Nestlé was established by Henry Nestlé in 1866 and it produces more than 8,000 lines of food products. It has established its manufacturing units in 197 countries. Its headquarters are in Vevey, Switzerland, and nearly three and a half lakh workers are employed there. Even today, it is one of the largest food companies in the world.

The status symbol of the wealthy is the Rolex watch. In 1905, Hans Wilsdorf, who was running a clock business in London, established this company. He was just twenty-four years old. In 1926, the Rolex Watch Company manufactured a waterproof watch and many international sportspersons have become its brand ambassadors since then. Its headquarters are in Geneva, Switzerland and nearly forty thousand people are employed by the company.

I studied the history of companies like these and their founders and discovered many trade secrets. However, I didn't keep these secrets with myself, but shared them with those who worked with me. I imparted my knowledge to everyone, to motivate them to work intelligently and make the company reach great heights.

As the saying goes, 'you reap what you sow'—and I reaped what I sowed. I was promoted to the position of area manager at an early stage in my sales career, even when my seniors were waiting to be promoted. The company increased my salary from Rs 10,000 to Rs 13,000 per month. My strategy, as you've just seen, was simple: to enjoy my work while working hard, to ask relevant questions so as to do better business, to understand people, to work effectively and learn from achievers who had made it big, worldwide.

Therefore, we see that one can achieve the best results if one enjoys what one does. There are two principles that one can follow to achieve results: the first one is, 'If you enjoy what you do, you don't have to work too hard to achieve results.' The second one is, 'If you do something you do not enjoy, you may mess up things and your life too.'

Every morning, if you enthusiastically get out of bed when you think of the day's work and happily set out to execute all that you have to do, then you are really enjoying your work.

A friend's son who is an avid footballer, enjoys his game of football. Though he failed to make a career as a footballer or to get a government job through the sports quota, he currently enjoys his job as a centre manager in a company that operates five-a-side football matches in the country. He enjoys coaching teams, organizing matches and bringing in revenue for his company. I also know many youngsters who followed their passion for music, film direction or law and built successful careers. Sometimes, people have jobs that they do not enjoy and they end up doing their work like a routine, without any achievements. A friend's father worked in a nationalized bank as a clerk and it took him several years to become a branch manager, because his development on the job was driven only by time-bound promotions. He chose voluntary retirement long before his superannuation and simply sat at home, taking care of his grandchildren. He regrets that he could never achieve great things, like establishing a school for children! But, in my case, I pursued my career with passion and enjoyed what I did. I was able to establish my identity in the company while getting promoted ahead of turn!

There are people who make their jobs interesting, even though they may have started accidentally. This is also how an interest in mathematics could be built in children who hate it, with stories and interesting problems. Many fear the popular train problems in algebra, but story problems have always engaged children. Thus, even a boring job can be made interesting with the right approach.

People are assets and I refer to them as human capital. Understanding them and their psyche can lead to result-oriented interactions in business. The fact that I shared my incentives with my fellow employees in the distribution network caught everyone's attention. In those days, an officer on the rolls of a company like Godrej Soaps was a rarity. The rest of the sales employees were employed by the distributors and their pay was much lower than that of those working for the company. No officer of the company ever shared his incentives with the distributors' salesmen and this act of mine indeed was an exception. I was genuinely concerned about the less privileged and sharing my earnings with them led to a close bond among members of the team and produced otherwise unachievable results.

This reminds me of a group activity on behavioural skills. A trainer gives each participant an inflated balloon. He asks each one of them to write their names on it, using an indelible pen. The trainer then gathers all the balloons, puts them in a room and asks the participants to find the one with their name on it, within five minutes. There is utter pandemonium in the room as everyone tries to find their own balloon. No one manages to find their balloon in the given time. Now, the trainer asks them to collect any balloon randomly and give it to the person whose name is written on it. Within a few minutes, each one is in possession of the balloon with their own name written on it. This attitude of giving and sharing is scarce and because of this, poor results are produced.

My gesture of sharing earned me many friends at work: distributors, shopkeepers, salespeople and delivery boys who, even today, remember me for my magnanimity and my sustained relationship with them.

There is a famous saying in retail: 'retail is detail'. And, smaller retail means smaller details. This is what I sought to address while interacting with small retailers. Alongside this, I was also studying successful businesses at a global level as I was keen to understand how they became successful.

If we thoroughly enjoy what we do, we don't have to work too hard to achieve results. We also have to ask the right questions to understand a business. Businesses are made up of people and understanding them helps us to have meaningful interactions which lead to success. We need to be inspired by achievers who have made it big in business across the whole world. And finally, we need to have an eye for detail! All these illustrations go to show that fortune truly favours those who work hard!

7

STEERING YOUR BOAT: ONLY YOU CAN

You steer your destiny!

Life is like sailing in a boat; family life is like having all the members of a family in the same boat! The idiom 'sailing in the same boat' means that everyone is in the same situation. Family members go through similar problems, whether financial or otherwise. But the head of the family has to steer the boat successfully. My mother did it for our family and she equipped us with the right qualifications to face the world. When my mother finally yielded to our request and came over to Chennai, she came with a heavy heart, as she had to leave her near and dear ones behind.

She adjusted well to life in Chennai. I was doing well in my career at Godrej and my mother thought that it was time for me to get married, so she told that I should get a permanent transfer to the city, as she liked the idea of having all her children around her again, just like we had all lived together in Nazareth!

Expectations from Marriage

I, however, had different expectations from marriage. I was aware of the traditions followed in Tamil Nadu, particularly in the southern regions, and I preferred something different. I shared these views with my mother, while assuring her that I would marry only when I found someone who matched these expectations.

While choosing a girl for marriage, it is common for the elders to give priority to material matters. But I wanted my elders to be different and consider my expectations for my prospective spouse. My expectations were simple. I wanted her to be God-fearing and to be prepared to share my life, which I knew would be a long journey ahead. Though I felt that I had outstanding talents and skills, I knew that I would not be promoted very far in the company. This was because only those with an MBA from reputed institutions managed to go higher, especially beyond certain levels, as a policy. So, I knew that I would not be promoted to a post which matched my skills. And, since I had been gaining experience rapidly in FMCG sales, I was ready to start my own business. Hence, I had planned to resign from my job in a few months, after my marriage. So, I wanted a wife who would not oppose such a bold move.

Starting a business is not just about reaping the joys of its ultimate success but it also poses the risk of losses. Since I would have to work pretty hard through the days ahead, I wanted my future wife to be willing to accept this and support me. She would also have to be prepared to face the various hardships that we might have to encounter together. Whatever the difficulties, I wanted someone who would not whisper them outside the four walls of my home and bear them with courage and a smiling face. These were some of the expectations that I had of my future wife.

Most girls lead a pretty comfortable life with their parents before marriage. After marriage, they expect the same comfort in their husband's home and, if these expectations are not fulfilled, they feel dejected; as a result, the marriage goes through turmoil. So, it was my wish that my wife should not have too many high hopes and would be a strong support in my journey towards fulfilling my goal. I firmly believed that only I would be able to choose a wife who would fulfil all these expectations.

Setting out to Find a Bride

With this in mind, I set out by car from Tirunelveli to meet Thelma, the great-granddaughter of the popular Abraham Pandithar of Tanjore. I was accompanied by a few relatives, Victor, his wife Chandra, Grace and Anbu. They said that Abraham Pandithar's family was renowned for its music and food. Anyone who visited their home received a warm welcome and delicious food. The women of this family, I was told, excelled in cooking and hospitality. On our way, I also learnt a lot about Thelma, that she had gone to school at St Peter's Primary School in Tanjore and later at the Women's Christian Higher Secondary School and had studied home science. I was curious to know why she'd chosen this subject, so I interrupted the conversation to ask, and received quite a stunning answer. Thelma loved cooking, but her mother had been firm that she would enter the kitchen only after completing college. Since Thelma did not intend to wait so long, she enrolled in the home science course because it would give her the opportunity to cook. I heard that she'd become an expert cook. I was assured by everyone that I would not have to worry about good food, as she would prepare sumptuous meals for me.

Thelma's parents were Mr Kanakarathina Pandian and Mrs Rani Pandian. They had five daughters and Thelma was the eldest. Since they had to marry them off one by one, they had begun to seek an alliance for Thelma when she was just twenty years old. A few wealthy families had sought her hand in marriage because of her good family background, but nothing had materialized for some reason or the other. So, Thelma waited for God's will to prevail.

On hearing about my intended visit, I later heard that Thelma prayed as usual and, this time, a verse from the Bible gave her a positive feeling. She was convinced that I was the man for her. Thelma was thrilled but also worried; on one hand, she was eager to see her future husband and on the other hand, she knew that as the first son-in-law in a family of five daughters, I would be expected to be like a son to the family. I would have to set an example for the other sons-in-law to come. Her major concern was whether I would be up to this.

The Meeting, the Realization and the Marriage

I met Thelma, along with my relatives, in an ice cream parlour in Trichy where the event of 'seeing each other' was arranged. A personal one-to-one meeting was not allowed in those days. It was love at first sight! I immediately expressed my willingness to marry her and so did she. I returned to Chennai to meet my mother and recounted my experience of 'seeing the bride', and concluded that I liked the girl. My mother was thrilled that I had decided to marry the very first girl I met. She was confident that I had chosen the right girl with God's guidance.

She immediately told everyone that we were going to proceed with this alliance. In the next few hours, the entire family received this happy news. The elders of our family congratulated me and wanted to know all the details about the bride. I also showed them Thelma's photo which I had got from her.

Marriage is a strong bond. It is God who decides who is meant for who. Thelma felt that a boy chosen by God would give her the garland of love. Our marriage was solemnized with the blessings of our families in December 1983. God blessed us and united us. Thelma became Mrs Padmasingh Isaac. Friends and relatives wished us a sweet and long wedded life.

We started our journey back to Chennai and, in Thelma, I saw all the excitement of the world! But she never guessed that, one day, she would face huge challenges in Chennai, that she would travel with her children in a crowded bus in a congested city and that she would have to run the family with meagre monthly funds, sometimes by pawning her jewellery. That's why experienced people call life an unfathomable mystery.

Marriage was a wonderful experience for both of us. We had come from different backgrounds, different families, different places, but stepped into our own family life, holding hands with the decision, 'From now on, we are one!'

Adjusting and Empowering

Thelma was awestruck by the tall buildings and busy life of Chennai. She would be living in a big city, leading quite a mechanical life. She became conscious of modern working women, vehicles plying at lightning speeds and jam-packed buses in the city. Initially, Thelma was quite bewildered by these confusing sounds and sights.

She began to hear other languages in the neighbourhood, apart from Tamil and English. Hearing Hindi, Telugu, Malayalam, Kannada and Urdu made her wonder if, indeed, this was the capital of just Tamil Nadu!

Her life in Tanjore had, on the contrary, been very quiet. Only Tamil was heard everywhere and English was rare. The sari was her favourite outfit, though occasionally she did wear a churidar-kurta and she'd never gone out alone.

Here in Chennai, women went everywhere alone and managed everything by themselves. Women, she found, enjoyed an equal status and had the capacity to compete against men. They ran to board buses; they drove two-wheelers and cars; they worked hard. All this terrified Thelma, but I understood her bewilderment and decided to remove that fear.

I asked her to prepare a list of things that she needed for the house. I then told her to hop on my bike and, halting near a big shop, I gave her some money and said, 'I'll be here; you go in and buy the things you need.' Thelma went in hesitantly. She returned with a heavy load of things and a bigger load of confidence. She went to the next shop to buy a few more things. Thus, I managed to get her accustomed to Chennai. Initially, I sent her to shops which were not crowded, where she bought things and hurried back. Then, slowly, I sent her into crowded shops. Here, she was initially confused, but I asked her to watch how other women bought things. She watched from a distance, till I asked her to go in and take a closer look, and she found that she could easily adjust to the situation. I took her to the shops for a few days and, after that, she gained the courage to go everywhere and do everything on her own.

Then, as the next step, I took her to bus stops during office hours, where working women stood among the crowds. The moment they saw a bus, these women would charge, holding on to their handbags. The bus would be full, with people packed like sardines. Despite that, the entire crowd from the bus stop would barge into a bus! Thelma was shocked to see all this; it was another world for her.

She pitied the women in the buses who were crushed and squeezed between other people. She realized that every woman had a family and everyone had to work. If they missed the bus, they would have to wait a long time for the next one; if they wanted to wait for an empty bus, they would always find a new crowd gathering at the bus stop. She understood that nothing could be accomplished in Chennai by waiting. Somehow, one had to seize the moment and move!

I taught her everything that she needed to learn. I showed her women who drove cars, women who went to banks, women who went for walks by themselves and so on, and told her that this was how she would have to learn to stand on her feet. It was the women of Chennai who gave her courage and self-confidence. She was also highly impressed by the women who ran businesses amidst so many men. The women who ferried their children on their two-wheelers amazed her. She also came across many women who finished all their chores at home, sent their children to school, dressed up and hurried to their office. They are the icons of Chennai. On seeing them, she developed courage and self-confidence.

Thelma learnt to adjust to Chennai life faster than I thought she would, while the city taught her a number of lessons!

Generally, if someone assumes that they know everything, they become conceited. They feel that there is nothing new to be learnt. Their over-confidence becomes apparent in their attitude, but Thelma was never showy or arrogant. She had genuine interests. So, she learnt all the good things and led a good life.

Today, as thousands of women from all over India come to Chennai, Thelma shares a lot of useful information with them to enhance their knowledge and awareness.

Taking Responsibility

Within a month, Thelma learnt to lead an independent life. So, we shifted to a separate house in Vaikakaran Street in Purasawalkam. Our first house was a rented one. It had two bedrooms and was on the second floor. Our monthly rent was Rs 300 and I had to pay an advance of Rs 5,000. In those days, I used to give money to my family, so we had quite a few monetary needs. We had to be frugal, otherwise we would have had to borrow.

In a situation where money was scarce, I taught Thelma the art of bargaining. Yet, I instructed her to never bargain with two categories of people. Compassion and kindness lay behind this instruction. The first were the women who sold flowers and the second, the ones who sold keerai (greens). The lives of most of these women were miserable. They suffered a lot and could get no other work. They took loans of Rs 100 or 200, paying a heavy interest, to enter this business. Their daily needs could be more than the profit that they could get from selling flowers. In most cases, a woman sold flowers and ran the household singlehandedly. Many of these women also had to support irresponsible husbands. Though their lives were sad, they had to do their work with a smile, to make a good impression on customers.

The women who sell keerai also come from difficult

backgrounds. They cannot sell the greens in large quantities, as they would wilt, which meant that their profits were not very high. I would see them walk on the streets wearily, longing for someone to buy their greens.

After I told her about these women, Thelma developed a soft corner for them and regularly bought flowers from them. She also told family members and acquaintances to never bargain with these women and, from then on till today, she continues to help them.

This is how a small-town girl adjusted to a big city.

As I have described, I planned my life, oriented towards my future. I had made up my mind to start a business, so I planned my family life in such a way that I would be fully supported by everyone around me. I did not express these ideas to anyone in the family, as elders may have objected to the idea of resigning from a promising job in a good company like Godrej. So, I kept these thoughts to myself as I looked for a humble wife who would identify with my ideals and would help me to achieve my goals. I hoped that my wife would share my vision for the future and would work with me through the ups and downs to achieve my goals.

I found all these qualities in Thelma and said 'yes' to her immediately. I wanted to lead my family along the right way from the very beginning. I was all set to take the driver's seat to steer my family life into a beautiful future. Thelma was a suitable partner for me and our match was made by God. She was indeed godsend for me! In body, mind and spirit, we became one.

I foresaw my prospects of growth in Godrej. I knew that I could grow in the organization only up to a certain extent. But, I knew my potential and I wanted to realize it. I yearned to grow by establishing a successful business. In pursuit of this dream, I made my plans. I decided that I would resign from my job one day, while I was on a 'good wicket' in the organization.

I helped my wife to adapt to life in the city. I empowered a woman brought up in a small town, to become independent and to build enough courage to face a big, busy city! This helped Thelma to understand her role in my life and even train other women in later years. I chose to empower my wife and taught her to be independent. Had I decided to do everything myself, restricting Thelma to the kitchen because she was from a small town, she would not have learnt anything in life!

This story of empowerment reminds us of the famous story of the butterfly in the cocoon and its fruitful struggle. A boy watched a butterfly struggling very hard to come out of its cocoon. It seemed that it was impossible for the butterfly to break free. The cocoon did not open up and the butterfly struggled harder, making very slow progress. It was desperate to break out of the cocoon. The boy was concerned and decided to help the butterfly. He gently tore open the cocoon to ease the butterfly out. The butterfly fell out, its body swollen and wings shrivelled. The boy thought that the butterfly would be fine as soon as it dried up but it never did. It crawled around with its deficiencies, and it could never become the beautiful fluttering butterfly that it ought to have been. Later, when the boy told his mother what he had done, he realized that a butterfly needs to struggle and break free in order to make its wings strong and beautiful!

In Chennai, my heart went out to the small vendors and hawkers. I restrained my wife from bargaining with them. I knew what hardships they went through to make both ends meet. My concern for these small vendors stemmed from my experience of having met many of them through my work. I wished that the philosophy of compassion would thrive in everyone. Not only did I practise this in my life, but I also made it a point to share it with my wife so that she too supported the hard-working women around her. She imbibed this quality, which provided a golden opportunity for her to engage the maximum number of disadvantaged women when she later set up her manufacturing facilities.

Preparing my life partner for the long haul was one of the key factors of my success. If steered ably, a boat navigates well and reaches its destination!

Know your true potential and plan your career accordingly. If you do not have the right qualifications to grow in what you currently do, make alternative plans to go where you can find growth. Engage yourself in activities that can help you realize your true potential. Realize that you have to prepare the people around you and empower them so that they can tune into your vision. It is often struggles that make people come out with flying colours! Finally, help those around you who toil hard and support them in the simplest ways you can. That is the first step you can take to practise social responsibility.

8

LEADING THE WAY BEFORE SHOWING THE WAY

When you lead, others follow!
There's a famous Chinese proverb that says, 'Tell me and I'll forget; show me and I may remember; involve me and I'll understand.' A 'telling leader' (pun intended) explains what he teaches and the student may absorb everything well, but only for a little while. A 'guidepost leader' shows the way, like a guidepost which shows the way but does not go with the traveller. The most important trait of effective leadership is the ability to involve everyone completely in their work. The 'engaging leader' gets things done efficiently, again and again, because his followers acquire the leader's expertise completely, in the way that he's taught them.

Leading by Example

I have always wanted to be No. 1 in everything I do. As an area manager of the company, I was fully committed to my work and travelled to sell the new products from my company. As I mentioned earlier, whenever my company introduced a new product, we opened special counters in important parts of the city. People were attracted to the counters where we screened commercial video and audio clippings. After this, each product was explained to the customers, highlighting its special features, qualities, benefits, cost, etc. The new product was compared to an existing corresponding product manufactured by a rival. During this time, I had to work round the clock.

I am going to again talk about the day I asked Thelma if she wanted to go to the counter. If you remember, I had taken her on my motorcycle and kept her by my side at the counter, even while I was busy attending to customers and she began to observe what was happening. Since it was a reputed company and the product was given a good deal of publicity, a large number of people crowded around the counter. They wanted to know details about the soap. I was answering every query patiently. Thelma watched me welcome the customers and patiently handle them by explaining everything to them clearly and calmly.

Respect Your Customer

That was, I had mentioned, Thelma's first business experience! It helped her learn how people were different from each other and what type of questions would be raised when a new product was introduced in the market and how they should be handled patiently. That day, after closing the counter and settling everything, we left for home. Thelma gently asked me how I stopped myself from getting angry when so many women repeatedly asked so many questions.

I replied to her, 'Gandhiji has said that customers are like gods. Though we may not think of them as gods, we should consider them to be our friends. When we consider someone to be our enemy, we could be annoyed by whatever they say. But, when we see them as our friends, we don't get angry, but will explain everything. I consider all my customers to be my friends, and give a lot of importance to women. So, I never get angry when they ask me any questions. And this is what my company pays me to do, expecting me to work with excellence.'

Then, I reminded her about the man we had seen at the entrance to the VGP Amusement Park, firm in his statue-like stance. She remarked that the 'statue man' did not move even during thunder and lightning. I told her that, likewise, even if others trouble us, we should remain unaffected.

I said, 'Of course, there are people who test our patience. Instead of losing our temper, we should handle them patiently, thinking that God has sent them to us to train us to control our anger. Most of the weapons that we use against our enemies would be enough to finish them; but if we use the weapon of anger against our enemies, it would boomerang and attack us. When we yell in anger, our blood circulation becomes irregular and our heart begins to palpitate. Our muscles become rigid and our eyes could pop out. Our whole body becomes imbalanced and stiff. Then, adrenalin rushes in. It is like setting fire to our own body. Having a short temper could reduce our lifespan. If short-tempered people see their faces in a mirror, they would despair. Losing one's smile makes one look old. Various health problems can also crop up because of excessive anger and force people to take medicines all their life. Hence, to retain our youth and health, we should avoid getting angry.' As I calmly explained, Thelma listened to me patiently.

Convince Yourself before Convincing Others

That day, we reached home at eleven in the night. The moment we entered the house, as I mentioned before, I hurried to the bathroom, with the newly introduced soap. I also took a coloured shirt and a white one with me.

Bewildered by this sight, Thelma wondered why I was doing so, when it was she who had been washing my clothes. So, she called out to me to stop washing clothes and go to bed, as she was concerned about me going to work the next day.

I told her, 'I have made all the customers believe that this soap is excellent; tomorrow I will be saying the same thing. But, before that, I would like to personally know the nature of this soap. Only then can I sleep peacefully. That's why I want to use it myself and test its quality.' I washed the two shirts separately and dried them.

I continued, 'I have given this soap to all those who work under my supervision. They will use it with water from their respective areas. Tomorrow morning, I will ask them their opinion about the soap. Before that, I should test the product myself, to find the actual quality of the product and be very clear that any product given by me to the people is of a good quality. If I have a negative result, I will write to my higher authorities about it.'

Thelma was amazed to hear this and she agreed with my conviction to check the quality of the product, before selling it to my customers.

In this chapter, I talk about a day when I had to organize 'spot sales', as we used to call them in FMCG parlance. These sales counters were usually demonstrative in nature: if there are food products, cooked samples are distributed to customers for tasting. For other products, the features, advantages and benefits are presented through storyboards and by personal selling and recommendations. Free offers and give-away items accompany sales, to entice customers to make instant purchases.

These spot sales were usually organized in the entrance area of a busy store, where the footfall was high. For newly launched products, this technique worked wonders. The company's salespeople took these products off the store shelves and arranged them on a table, accompanied by product props and storyboards. The stalls were decorated with festoons and buntings and manned by sales staff attired in identical clothes that bore the relevant product and brand communication. At the end of the day, the company's salespeople would settle the stock and cash account with the store owner from whose store they had pulled out the stocks. Then, they moved on to the next location, so that a wide area would be covered for initializing product trials for potential customers.

Small store owners were always happy about such product demonstrations as these FMCG companies drew people to their stores and consequently they ended up achieving higher sales. They also made an effort to facilitate larger sales of the demonstrated products, which eventually brought repeat customers to them. As an area head, I was responsible for organizing many spot sales counters. The usual responsibility of the area managers was to ensure smooth and timely operations at these spot sales counters. I was different in my way of working. I made sure that I was standing by my colleagues and participating in these demonstration sales. I sold the products by interacting with customers, understanding their needs and getting their feedback to optimize our and selling strategies. The style of leadership that I practised was uniquely participative. My leadership guru has always been John C. Maxwell, who is the foremost authority on leadership in the world today. I often remind everyone of Maxwell's famous leadership quote, 'A leader is one who knows the way, goes the way and shows the way.' It reiterates the three most important points to take cognizance of. First, that leadership is understanding—knowing what to do and how to do it. Second, that leadership is demonstration—the leader has to do any task himself, to practically experience the nuances of what is to be done and how it can be done. Third, that leadership is guidance—the leader has to guide the ones who follow. Unless the first two are followed, 'showing the way' can never be achieved. I am a strong proponent of the theory of 'leading the way' myself before 'showing the way' to my colleagues. My act of using the soap I was selling exemplifies all the three aspects depicted in Maxwell's popular leadership adage: knowing the way, going the way and showing the way! I also took my wife along with me and showed her the way and she learnt that the conviction to win over a situation comes with personal experience.

> *Don't be a guidepost that can only show the way, but a leader who can go along with followers and show them the way. So, 'go the way' before you 'show the way'. Next, consider customers to be your friends and you will never be angry or upset with them, come what may; they are the ones who are your paymasters. Also, control your anger and every situation will be positive. Don't forget to internalize your own product or service by experiencing it yourself, before you recommend it to your customers. And, last but not the least, you are convincing to others only when and if you are ready to personally go through the same experience.*

> *Remember to follow the principle, 'lead, before, you show!'*

9

CHARTING A NEW COURSE: THE TURNING POINT TO SUCCESS!

No time?

'Lazy fellows, who don't plan for anything and therefore have no plan to follow, are the ones who don't have the time to do not only the necessary things, but also their daily duties. But, active people never have the problem of "no time". Now that I am sixty plus, I am more active than I was before and I have travelled nearly two lakh miles across the country, inaugurating many exhibitions, serving in national organizations and campaigning for self-sufficiency. I have been to Europe twice. Yet, all these activities have never come in the way of my scientific research. I have reduced my holidays and continued with my research,' said P.C. Ray, an eminent Indian scientist.

Inspired by Mr Ray, I always keep myself active and busy.

Financial Needs Are a Good Impetus to Change Course

My elder son, Ashwin Pandian, was born in October 1984. As

my family began to grow, my responsibilities and duties as a husband and father grew as well. Though the family expenditure was increasing, my salary remained the same. As I wondered how I was going to meet the financial needs of my family, I started thinking about starting my own business. But the situation was not conducive for the change and days went by without a concrete decision. When Ashwin was two years old, Thelma conceived again and Abishek Abraham was born in September 1986 in Tanjore. The family, thus, grew to four members.

Owing to the extra needs of the little ones, the need for money increased. All I knew was to work hard. I worked hard day and night, achieved my targets and earned commissions. Whenever I earned a commission, I would share it with my team because it was teamwork that made it possible to achieve the target. Finally, I came home with almost nothing in hand. All I got from the job was the satisfaction I gleaned from my hard work and from achieving my targets.

I reduced my personal expenses and handed over a large portion of my salary to Thelma. In those days, my eldest sister Saroja Paul Devaraj was running a chit fund within a circle of family members, with monthly instalments of Rs 200 and Rs 500 every month. Thelma joined this fund with the money she used to save from my salary. Though I was aware of this, I did not ask her about it. But, when my sister came home, I knew that she brought money from the fund. Both the children were growing up fast and needed more space to run around and play. Since there was a water scarcity during summer, we shifted to Anna Nagar and started living in an apartment near Chinmaya Vidyalaya, for a rent of Rs 500 per month.

Looking for Finance

The need for money increased day by day and my mind was full of business ideas. I finally decided to start my own business, if I could get the capital to invest in it. I needed quite a huge amount as an investment. My attempts to borrow money from people I knew failed miserably. Nobody actually refused to my face, but instead asked me to come back the next day. Some made excuses about wanting more information about the business I was planning to start. When I mentioned my proposed business, they said, 'This business is really not suitable for you at this point in time! Though I would like to give you a loan, what will happen if your business fails? Think of something else...' Like this, instead of bluntly refusing to give me a loan, people would beat around the bush, sometimes questioning my enthusiasm and trying to shatter my dreams.

I realized that most people were trying to smash my dreams to smithereens. So, I took this as a challenge and developed a burning passion to somehow start the business and run it successfully. Money was the only thing I needed! All I had to offer in exchange for a loan was hard work, a priceless commodity, but which no one seemed to think valuable.

Finance Was within Arm's Reach

This made me realize that the investment could come from only one place, my company! I remembered that my provident fund and benefits for several years of service would give me a helping hand. To get this, I would have to pay a heavy price: I would have to resign from my job which was giving my family a regular monthly income.

Making a mental calculation, I found out that my PF and gratuity would together fetch me Rs 80,000. But I was unsure how Thelma would react to this decision. I was certain that she would be shocked and terrified, not knowing how to run the family, which was already struggling to make ends meet, even with the monthly salary. I knew that if I told my mother, she would be in tears and would plead with me not to quit my job. So, I decided not to confide in anyone about my decision.

Taking Full Responsibility

I charted out a complete and detailed plan for my business. Thelma immediately sensed a difference in my behaviour. From the first days of our marriage, I had been running everywhere round the clock and would think twice about taking leave for a single day. But now, I was sitting at home for days, thinking about the business all the time. This increased her curiosity and finally she asked me if I wasn't going to work. I slowly told Thelma that I had quit my job six days ago. She was taken aback. She exclaimed in complete shock, 'What do you mean? We have to send our children to school, for which we need money; why have you done this, at this juncture?' Recovering from her shock, she asked, 'What do we do next?' She did not create a scene by raising her voice, neither did she complain to her mother-in-law or parents that her husband had done such a drastic thing.

This is what I expected from her. I sat her down and shared two important things with her.

First, I explained to her that we would progress and achieve a lot in life, but it would not be easy; we would have to work hard to fight for our success and I had no idea how long that fight would be. I told her that during the period of struggle, people could mock us and some would discourage us. We could even lose the Rs 80,000 that we had in hand for the business. This would be like entering a battlefield. So, she would have to be prepared for any eventuality, including embarrassing situations. Whatever happens, we should never step back. We should not be defeated and flee. Many had done so in a similar journey. They would advise us to run away, but we should not heed their advice and work hard to achieve what we want.

After that, I explained to her that, whatever the cost, our family, friends and relatives should not come to know about any hardship that we may suffer. Even our children should not know about it!

Thelma smiled at me, acknowledging that she understood. I asked in awe, 'How is it that you are able to smile even in this difficult situation?' She replied with another reassuring smile.

A decision to quit a well-paying and respectable job that came with a promise for the future was difficult to take, but I did it with hope. Thirty years ago, there were no funding options for start-up businesses, except to begin with the small savings accumulated over a period of time. Often, investing in a new business amounted to putting one's life's savings at risk. The money for the very first investment in my business was within my reach and I put my finger on it at the right time. Yes, it was from my statutory savings, like the PF and gratuity payable to me on quitting the job.

Though I had hopes of raising loans from my friends and relatives, I realized that I was far from getting any temporary credit from them. I had conviction in my plans but they refused to see my confidence and did not support me. Investing the little capital I had, I bootstrapped my business.

I thought of an innovative funding strategy. No one would have ever thought of raising funds from the savings created by a family-run chit fund. This became a constant source of funding for my business. The chit fund values would vary and I would subscribe to the group of my choice based on the affordable chit size. Whenever I required the money, I withdrew it in the auction. During those days, access to initial funding was a major challenge for start-up entrepreneurs like me, as banks and non-banking financial companies (NBFC) were hesitant to lend money. Besides, globalization had not happened and the concept of an open economy was just a dream. Many start-up businesses were proprietary in nature. The limited access to financial assistance was in the form of bank loans and money could be raised by pledging jewellery or by mortgaging property. This was in addition to access to funds from periodical savings, like chit funds. All these were the traditional ways of funding a start-up business, and I used all these means to raise money as a first-generation entrepreneur.

Conviction is perhaps what has made me who I am today. I had a strong conviction, which others could not see, in my own abilities to succeed in business. I made efforts to access investment. I dipped into my small savings and utilized the money wisely to implement my business plan.

I told my wife that success was a sure end to the hardship which we would suffer. But, come what may, the sufferings had to be confined within our home. I said this because I did not want to be affected by any negativity from the discouragement of our near and dear ones.

It is now worthwhile to remember the popular story of the

two frogs that fell into a deep well. One made it to freedom by jumping out and the other stayed in the well and died. As a group of frogs hopped through the wilderness, two of them fell into an abandoned well. When the other frogs saw the depth of the well, they shouted at the top of their voices to both the frogs that they were in a very deep well and would never be able to come out. While both the frogs tried to jump out of the well, the frogs outside continued shouting that it was useless to try. Despite that the frogs tried to jump out of the well, until one listened to the crowd outside and gave up. It fell back and died eventually. The other frog tried harder to jump out of the well and it did come out finally! When the frog made it outside, the other frogs asked how it had done so.

The frog that had jumped out turned out to be deaf! It had not heard the voices of the other frogs! This illustrates that turning a deaf ear to the negative voices of those around us can help us achieve what we plan to do. So, I was wise enough to keep all our struggles within the home so that we did not expose ourselves to any negative forces that could pull us down.

Charting the path of establishing a new business, when I had the option of being employed in an organization, was a difficult one. But I decided to go for it and that made all the difference. My decision concurs with what Robert Frost reflects in the concluding lines of his poem, 'The Road Not Taken'.

Two roads diverged in a wood, and I—
I took the one less travelled by,
And that has made all the difference!

Look around you for resources and they will become available to you; deploy innovative thinking to fund your business. Keep hardships close to your heart so that you can learn from them. Have conviction in your plan and tell yourself and those around you that you will succeed. We should take the right decision at the right time, even if it means charting a totally new course to become successful. Finally, like the frog, turn a deaf ear to negative voices and you will succeed.

10

BEFRIENDING FAILURES, THE STEPPING STONES TO SUCCESS

Face failures without fear Fear is what you should fear! Making mistakes and facing failures should not be something we should be afraid of: They should be faced. As long as we are bold enough to face failures, we will be achievers. Achievers are schooled by mistakes and study in the college of failures. Then and only then do they succeed in learning the lessons of life.

I have made many mistakes and they have cost me quite a lot. I was dejected by these failures. If I had run away from them out of fear, I would have been a failure throughout my life. Using the lessons that I learnt from my mistakes and failures, I fought to succeed. So, if mistakes and failures are not there in life, we will not learn anything.

A Business Idea Crystallizes

I had always liked wearing white shirts and I used liquid blue to keep my shirts white and clean. This practice made me start my first manufacturing business.

In those days—around 1985—Robin Blue from the then Reckitt & Coleman was sold as a powder and another brand was sold in the form of a liquid. But these were sold in 50 ml and 100 ml packages. So, I decided to produce high-quality liquid blue in smaller quantities and market it.

I knew the method for producing liquid blue, but I still had to carry out practical tests to find out the exact proportion of raw materials to create a successful product. I rented a house for this purpose and used one room to test my product.

Every day, from morning to night, I would boil the raw materials and create a formula. Once the product was ready, I used to test its quality on several white clothes. Satisfied with the outcome, I would give it out to the neighbours and request them to use it and give me their feedback. I would listen to their opinion patiently. It took me three months to be satisfied with its quality to some extent, after listening to the reports from the women who used it. Quite a lot of money was spent on these tests. Yet, I was not ready to manufacture it till I got a 100 per cent positive feedback about my product. Finally, I created what I decided was a quality product and called it Twinkle Blue!

Packed in attractive vials with striking stickers, Twinkle Blue shone brightly. It was made available in packs of 5 ml and 10 ml. I became an all-rounder who made the product, marketed it and collected the money. I had one assistant to help me, for whom I rented a room, where I also produced and bottled the liquid blue.

I went through all the anxiety that a start-up businessman faces. The products of my previous company were famous and, hence, I did not have any difficulty in marketing them. I had mastered the art of selling by creating an interest among shopkeepers and making them buy the products in bulk. Despite my capabilities and my acquaintance with the shopkeepers, they hesitated to buy the liquid blue from me.

The Problems Begin

The shopkeepers, who had warmly welcomed me earlier, when I had been working for Godrej, ignored me when I went with my own brand, avoiding me with lame excuses. Many of them never even gave me a chance to tell them about the quality of my product. But I don't have any regrets. I knew pretty well that anyone starting a new venture would be treated with indifference, but I had the confidence that the same indifference would, one day, make me an achiever. Therefore, I was not disheartened by this; I vowed to create something that would make the same people who shunned and dodged me now, invite me in willingly.

I never blamed the retailers for taking time to place their confidence in me, but encouraged myself by saying that it was a new product and that was the reason they didn't trust it yet, but that as soon as they gained confidence, they would buy my products.

At the same time, since shopkeepers refused to buy my liquid blue, I could not pay the suppliers of the raw materials. Even the few shopkeepers who bought the liquid blue, returned it saying that it did not sell. My suppliers began to pressurize me for the money I owed them. While wondering how to manage this situation, another problem cropped up. One of the suppliers cheated me by supplying poor-quality raw materials instead of the high-quality raw materials that I needed and had paid for. Since I was not aware of this initially, plenty of liquid blue was produced with that kind of material. When I came to know that it was of a poor quality, I did not want to sell, so I threw all of it away and incurred a huge loss.

Debts Start Piling up

By this time, the Rs 80,000, which I had begun with, had gone. All the gold and jewellery belonging to Thelma were pledged. To keep my promise to my debtors and to save my honour and dignity, we decided to pledge her mangalsutra, the wedding chain. Thelma knew quite well the distress of a married woman without her mangalsutra, and she hesitated to face people without it. At times, she didn't know what to say when someone asked her about her missing mangalsutra. It was a big challenge for her to hide this from her relatives. But, this soon became a minor worry as other problems came our way.

The debts kept rising and, not knowing what to do, we tried to save money by joining the monthly chit fund, which became a way of life for us. As the financial crisis intensified, I felt the signs of failure looming closer.

Different people have different views about this enemy called failure. Some see it as a mythical monster, some as a huge dinosaur from *Jurassic Park*, fuelled by the idea that 'failure is stronger and bigger than me'. This attitude leads people to accept failure and feel dejected, which means that failure soon overpowers them. Then, there is nothing left for them but to join the list of those who have failed.

Not Intimidated My Failure

I did not let failure affect me. My attitude differed from that of most others. Taking lessons from previous experiences, I boldly ventured into the field to fight failure.

My idea was unique; I did not consider failure to be a foe, but a friend. So, instead of hating it, I enjoyed it. As a result, I was not afraid of it, but approached it with a positive attitude.

I realized that if I failed in business, it was entirely because of my own mistake. It was meaningless to blame others and try to shift the responsibility. So, I introspected and found that the fault lay in the raw materials that had sunk me into debt; I blamed myself for not testing the raw materials properly.

When I was in this terrible financial crisis, I often bought raw materials on credit, so the supplier had decided to give me poor-quality material. But I realized this only after some time and I could not immediately make any alternative arrangements.

I wondered how I was going to come out of this crisis. Though I had lots of self-confidence, I called unto God to guide me. That morning, before starting my work, I began to pray, 'God, I am making all possible efforts. Please be with me and guide me.' After praying, I was hopeful that God would guide me out of this situation.

An Answer to my Prayer

God answered my prayer one day in 1990. Two merchants by the names of Parth and Rathore were introduced to me in Parry's Corner in Chennai. My education, experience, intelligent conversation and other qualities seemed to have appealed to them and both of them took me to their shop and treated me with respect. They said that they wanted to conduct business with me and that they were ready to supply any quantity of high-quality raw materials to me. I felt that I could trust these men and that they would supply good material to me, but the only problem was money.

Understanding my hesitation, the two businessmen said, 'You needn't worry about money; we're willing to give you raw materials on credit for a year. There is no need to give us any money now. After a year, you can give us the money. Until then, we will continue supplying you the materials.'

Thelma and I were thrilled by God's wonderful doing. We could not believe our ears and wondered whether it was a dream or reality.

We began to recover slowly and, as a gesture of support, my elder brother Augustine and my younger brother Topsingh redeemed Thelma's mangalsutra by paying Rs 35,000, for which we will always be grateful to them.

As soon as we had enough money, we settled the debt which we owed to the supplier of poor-quality raw materials. Relieved that this major problem had been solved, I chalked out a new plan. I recruited five new people: two of them would manufacture the liquid blue and the other three would distribute it to the shops, take orders and collect the money, on tricycles.

This professional plan, drawn from previous experience, is an excellent example for all those who want to start their own business. Normally, manufacturers supply their product through distributors to the shops, from where the shopkeepers sell it to customers. When a person starts his own business and introduces his product, shopkeepers do not accept it immediately. This is because they are doubtful of its quality, and even if they do believe it to be good, they need to create trust in their customers. It's only then that the customers buy the new product.

Most merchants do not have the time to explain anything about a new product in order to be able to convince customers to buy it. Hence, generally, they do not support new products.

This is the problem!

So, when I introduced my liquid blue, most shopkeepers were quite indifferent, yet some bought it. On hearing about this, reputed companies which were already selling liquid blue, indirectly threatened these shopkeepers, saying that they would stop supplies of their product if they bought the new brand.

Out-of-the-box Selling Strategies

When this happened, I decided to sell directly to the customers. It was my belief that, if I could prove my liquid blue's quality, then I would be able to make the shopkeepers come to me.

I executed my plan by targeting the markets. I explained the quality of my product and, as an introductory offer, I gave a stainless steel cup, bowl and box as freebies. To improve sales, I sold my product for a low price with a very narrow profit margin.

I knew that, once bought, there would be repeat purchases since it was of a good quality. Encouraged by this thought, I actively worked towards this, by meeting people directly and selling my product. After every month, I would move to continue my sales in a new place.

Those who used the liquid blue for the first time were satisfied by its quality and demand began to grow. In due course, the shopkeepers who had initially refused to buy my product, now approached me and requested me to supply it to their shops. I had achieved what I had wanted.

Going through the people in a particular area, I was able to influence the shopkeepers and, thus, my business strategy worked well and the business flourished.

This successful new business approach is, today, appreciated by many and is even followed by many businessmen.

I succeeded because of hard work, precise plans and dedication.

In the meantime, my landlord asked me to find another house and gave me a notice period of ten days to shift, as he needed the house immediately for his family.

A house had to be found immediately. A few days passed. The owner of the room, which I had rented for product development, visited me and gave me another shocking piece of news. He said that he needed the room for his personal use and gave me 15 to 20 days' notice to vacate the room.

Difficulties sometimes come in twos and threes! But, without any hesitation, I assured both men that I would vacate their places.

Turning Problems into Opportunities

With a big smile, I told Thelma that it was good that both problems had come together, thereby making things easy for us, since I wouldn't need to run around looking for two places. I would find just one place for living in, as well as to run the business from. But I knew that Thelma understood that I was trying to lighten the situation by cracking a joke.

I was determined to make liquid blue in bigger quantities than before and build a large-scale business. So, I looked for a bigger place to serve both as a residence and an office. We found such a house within two weeks. It was a single-bedroom house and we shifted in. Later, we decided to lease a 1,200 sq. ft. building in Thangam Colony, Anna Nagar for office use, for a rent of Rs 1,000. It was quite advantageous, having an office in the same area where one lived.

Adapting to the new environment, we worked cheerfully.

As promised, Parth and Rathore supplied good-quality raw materials and we were able to produce good-quality liquid blue and gradually the business picked up.

In his autobiography *My Experiments with Truth*, Mahatma Gandhi speaks about his first failure as a practising lawyer: 'This was my début in the Small Causes Court. I appeared for the defendant and had thus to cross-examine the plaintiff's witnesses. I stood up but my heart sank into my boots. My head was reeling and I felt as though the whole court was doing likewise. The judge must have laughed and the vakils (lawyers) no doubt enjoyed the spectacle. But I was past seeing anything. I sat down and told the agent I could not conduct the case.' During the first six months of his law practising career, he incurred more debts. At this stage of his life, according to biographer Judith M. Brown, Gandhiji was 'an Indian nonentity'. But Gandhiji's social walk of life made history across the world. He learnt from his experiences and motivated himself to be who he became, taking up the right causes to make a big difference!

My journey of entrepreneurship was no bed of roses either. But I took every challenge in my stride and converted challenges into opportunities. As I was tiding over financial challenges, other troubles mounted. The challenge I faced with the supplier of poor-quality raw materials, made me look for fresh sources of supply, which ultimately resulted in the development of a better product for the customer.

The next key challenge was in the marketplace, where shopkeepers did not welcome me with the same warmth as when I had been selling a reputed company's product. So, I worked on unique strategies, offering freebies and greater gross margin advantages, for shopkeepers to be motivated to sell Twinkle Blue. I hit upon the strategy of going directly to customers to promote the product, which created a demand for my product in the local market. I carefully treaded on troubled waters without losing sight of my entrepreneurial mission and I was determined to see opportunity in every calamity that hit me.

Even when my landlord asked me to vacate the premises from where I ran my business, I thought of it as an opportunity to move into a bigger place that would provide room for the expansion of my business.

Help came from God when I prayed to Him. My brothers and their timely help, coupled with the new suppliers of raw materials, Parth and Rathore, were indeed godsends!

I held on steadfastly to my spirit of entrepreneurship and clung to my gut feeling that my future was in business rather than in being an employee in someone else's company. So, I never ever thought about going back to work for a company, even with lucrative offers coming my way. Despite the rejection I faced from many people, I concentrated on succeeding in my business, truly living my long-cherished dream of becoming a successful businessman!

We all know of the famous Hershey's chocolates. The founder of Hershey's, Milton Snavely Hershey, was a school dropout at the age of fourteen. He developed an interest in candy-making and decided to work as an apprentice with a confectioner in Lancaster. Later, he borrowed some money from his aunt and set up his own candy shop in Philadelphia. Hershey put all his efforts into his business for five long years, but he did not meet with success, so he closed his shop. Reuniting with his father in Denver, he started working again with a confectioner there. He discovered caramel and found out how fresh milk could be used to make caramel chocolates. Since Hershey was never satisfied when working with someone, he wanted to be an entrepreneur again and his heart was set on establishing his own business. He established his chocolate business in Chicago and later in New York City. He failed at both locations. In 1883, he went back to Lancaster and, with a strong will to succeed in business, he established the Lancaster Caramel Company. Hershey's innovative thinking focused on producing and selling quality milk chocolate candy. It worked wonders and he became successful. In 1900, he sold the Lancaster Caramel Company for a whopping one million dollars. In 1905, he opened the most modern candy-making facility in Derry Church that set a new trend for the candy industry across the world! The huge impact of the company founded by Milton Hershey is felt even today.

Failures are just experiences from which one learns and they must not be feared. The anecdotes about Mahatma Gandhi and Milton Hershey tell us how they became great success stories. Had they been brooding on their pitfalls and failures, they would never have reached their destinations.

I treated failure not as an enemy but as a friend. I was not defeated by failure but I approached each failure with a positive attitude, to learn from it and make corrections. Thus, I enjoyed coming up with the right solution for each catastrophe that occurred. When I found the right solutions, I had my success stories to tell.

In a nutshell, we should learn to convert catastrophes into opportunities. We must realize that the first step to success begins with the decision to try and we must never fear failure and step back; failures precede every success. Remember that quality sells: The quality of a product is the backbone that supports a brand. Finally, you can bet even your last penny that, if you have a strong conviction, your venture will succeed!

11

THINK, IDEATE, INNOVATE AND CREATE A WHOLE NEW WORLD

Never judge another's abilities!

No one should try to judge the ability of another. I don't mean to disrespect teachers, but there are historical examples which prove that teachers have not always been able to evaluate a child's intelligence.

Albert Einstein was certified as the most unintelligent boy by one of his teachers who said, 'I have never seen such a rotten-brained student like him.'

The nickname given by a teacher to Thomas Alva Edison was 'Addled' (confused). Not stopping at that, the teacher dismissed Edison from school. But, later on, it was Edison who became the father of thousands of inventions.

The teacher who rebuked Einstein and the one who dismissed Edison might have appreciated several thousands of other students who never made a place for themselves in the annals of history. Those who think freely and differently become achievers. For them, a house must be like a church (not a prison), and a school must be like a park (not a fortress with restrictions). Create such an atmosphere for your child if you want him or her to become an achiever.

Women and Their Traditional Kitchen

The farming community is the backbone of India. Similarly, a woman is the backbone of every family. It is she who has the responsibility of safeguarding the health of each and every family member. It is she who has to choose the right food products, cook, serve the dishes with love and maintain the family's health. Women have many roles in life, as grandmother, mother, sister, wife and daughter, And they have different responsibilities in each role. Most women do their job to perfection.

I was born in a family of six children, brought up by my mother, taken care of by my grandmother, guided by my eldest sister and supported by my wife. This made me develop a special respect for women. I always made it a point to show respect to all of them. I want to give the same respect, which I gave to my mother, wife and sister, to all the unknown women in the far ends of the earth.

People used to believe that women were born only to cook. So, they confined women inside the four walls of the kitchen, for nearly the whole length of the day. Their daily work was mainly to cook food and serve it. Many a time, they waited at the kitchen door, eager to hear a word of appreciation for their cooking from the male members of their home.

Seeing the plight of these women, shut within the kitchen right from their puberty, several leaders gave a clarion call to empower them so that they could progress in life.

The Kitchen, a Prison

Following this, several changes took place. Women received education, gained knowledge and also joined politics. Yet, they were not liberated from the kitchen—instead, more responsibilities were heaped on them. They were made to balance both cooking and a career. Their plight had a great impact on me.

The kitchen, tiny in the early days, became larger later. Modern gadgets like grinders and mixers replaced early tools like pestles, pounders and grinders made of stone. Modern stoves were added. This did not change the condition of the women. They continued to be prisoners in a modern kitchen with modern gadgets.

Women are supposed to get up early in the morning, finish cooking, take care of the children, send them off to school and then get ready to go to work. Amidst all this, they have to buy things for the household, which is also a huge job. From the age of twenty-five, while visiting several shops to take orders for my company, I had keenly observed women buying things needed for cooking.

Women made a monthly list of things required for cooking, saved the required amount of money and went to different shops to buy the items. Let us look at the example of chilli powder. Women would check the quality and buy what they considered to be the best chilli and then dry it, preserve it and take it to the grinding shops to powder it. They would leave the powdered chilli to cool and then pack it tightly in small boxes to ensure that the powder did not get infested with insects.

All this effort was required to procure chilli powder for the kitchen. They also had to struggle to powder things like turmeric, coriander and fenugreek. The same procedure had to be followed for flour, rice, urad dal, grains, peanuts and so on.

I felt that this arduous work in the kitchen, after a long day at office, was a major task for them. This made me think.

Wasted Time and Poor-quality Products

When I roughly calculated how much time, effort and money a woman spent on getting a masala or flour made, I was shocked.

I also noticed another important thing. How will the women who bought these chillies or coriander know if they were of a good quality? There is no guarantee for the quality. Also, they needed to have the space to dry the chillies and guess whether the grinding place was clean and hygienic or not.

To buy all these masalas for a month's supply, they had to spend a considerable amount of money in one day. And to top it all, there is a vast difference in flavour and taste between the masalas ground immediately and the ones stored in a box for a whole month.

Indian masalas are some of the most excellent ones in the world because they have a wonderful aroma, which is the nice smell that we get from dried chillis, coriander, cardamom, cloves, etc. In order to retain this aroma, we need to grind spices in hygienic conditions using modern methods, pack them well to preserve them and take them to the kitchen from the shops. On the other hand, grinding spices and preserving them without a proper method result in a loss of their aroma. If the same masala is used to cook food, it would lose its flavour and nutritional value.

Unaware of these facts, women bought masalas, ground them without using a proper method and wasted their money and efforts, jeopardizing their health. I was concerned by this and finally decided to do something about it. I clearly understood that only when we reduce the time needed to prepare masalas, can we release women from the clutches of arduous cooking, and they will never be prisoners in the kitchen again. Only when women's time in the kitchen is reduced, will they be able to exhibit their skills and abilities in other fields. With time on their hands, they can use other opportunities and progress in life. And only when women progress, does the family progress; and finally, so does the nation.

At the same time, I knew the importance of cooking to produce healthy and tasty food at home. But, a whole hour did not need to be spent making pongal for five persons, if it could be done in just five minutes! I wondered if it was necessary to spend forty-five minutes on some curry or sauce, grinding, powdering and mixing a few masalas. It should be finished within three minutes! I also wondered what could relieve women from this strenuous work. I did not stop with just thinking about this but started formulating a plan which I could implement and, thereby, alleviate their plight.

Conducting a Survey and My Findings

I found that, on an average, a woman took seventy-five minutes to make a traditional breakfast for a family of four members. My goal was to reduce this time to fifteen minutes.

Here is a list of what I found in my survey.

1. In the 1990s, many shops sold ground masalas in desired quantities as sought by customers. These were not branded masalas. They were neither tested nor did they bear a trademark for quality. I realized that if quality masalas were used instead,

validated by proper testing and packed with a brand name, there would be a great improvement in people's health.

2. If the packed masalas were made in small packets for daily use, women would not need to spend a lot of money. Rather, they could buy packets for Rs 5 or Rs 10 and, in the small packets, the flavour and aroma of the masalas would be retained for a longer period.

3. Women usually have to add nearly ten different types of masalas to prepare a curry. They have to open ten boxes, take out each masala without spilling it and carefully close the boxes after. All this needs time, patience and careful handling. Even if one ingredient is forgotten, a lot of the taste is lost. If they add an extra ingredient or if they do not have one of them, again, the taste is spoiled.

   I realized that if the ten ingredients are mixed in the right proportion, ground and packed to retain the aroma, it would be very easy to make any curry without any confusion. There would not be any stress in the kitchen.

4. If all the ingredients of a masala were pre-mixed and packed, even women who do not know cooking would be able to cook easily.

5. If ready-mixed food products were sold in packets, women could prepare tasty food within minutes. Then, they would have plenty of time to do other things.

6. Knowingly or unknowingly, society brought inequality to food. There were certain dishes which could be consumed only by the rich at expensive hotels which could get them prepared and the poor could not afford to eat at these restaurants. Such dishes, I thought, should be made available even to ordinary people and, with this, discrimination between the rich and the poor could be reduced.

7. If tasty and high-quality food products are sold in packets and prepared at home, people would enjoy their taste and applaud the efforts of the women. This would strengthen marital and familial relationships. Children, too, would appreciate the mother's cooking and prefer it to eating at restaurants. Hence, restaurant food and expenditure could be avoided.

8. Diseases were on the rise and I knew that the number of diabetics in India was growing at such a rate that India would soon be called the diabetic capital of the world. Several people in India were also dying of cancer and many had heart diseases. I was convinced that it was very important to safeguard the health of India. People should have a balanced diet, be strong and have a good immune system. For this, branded food products of a high quality were essential.

9. For ages, women have cooked and prepared food. Since cooking was thought to be difficult, men hesitated to enter the kitchen. If cooking could be made easy, husbands would be willing to help the wife, and the son, his mother. This would bring about a great social revolution.

My education and practical knowledge helped me undertake this survey in the 1990s. I realized that if high-quality, hygienic and tasty food products provided an easy cooking experience, women and society would enjoy the rewards. So, I then entered the specialized area of creating convenience food products of high quality for easy cooking!

We have all heard of Henry Ford's vision of building a motor car that the common man could afford. This was at a time when cars were expensive and only the rich could afford them. To make affordable cars, Ford had to create a model that could be sold at an affordable price. In 1908, as a result of his continuous innovation, he developed the Model T, a car for the masses. He created an efficient process for manufacturing this new model so that prices could be brought down. At that time, the process of manufacturing cars was such that it took a long time to assemble one, just one car at a time. Productivity was at an ebb. Even after streamlining the existing method, a dramatic improvement in productivity was not achieved. He kept thinking and ideating on ways to increase speed and process efficiency in production so that the output could be improved. As he observed the manufacturing process more closely he found that the employees continuously moved around to attend to the various tasks of building the car. He remembered what he had observed in meat processing earlier, where the hanging carcasses moved on a conveyor belt above the stationary workmen, who did their job. He wondered why men should go to the task instead of the task coming to the men, to save time! His innovation changed the whole process of manufacturing, creating history in 1913. He invented the assembly line. The man-hours of final assembly were brought down from more than twelve hours to a mere 2.5 hours. That innovation resulted in the production of quality cars at a rapid pace. 'In 1912, Ford Motor Company produced 82,388 Model Ts, and the touring car sold for $600. By 1916, Model T production had risen to 585,388, and the price had dropped to $360. On 4 June, 1924, the 10-millionth Model T rolled off the Highland Park assembly line.'[1]

Henry Ford showed how thinking, ideating and innovating could have a huge impact on fulfilling the achievement of one's vision. Like Ford, I too desired to think and innovate. I thought

---

[1] https://media.ford.com

of the empowerment of women and wanted to save their time which could then be used fruitfully in other pursuits. Thinking, ideating and innovating can change people's lives, impact the growth of our business and even create a whole new world.

> *Talent and capability are inherently present in everyone, no one should be discarded as useless. Identify the specific problems that you have at hand, around you. Focus on them to find solutions and ideate through your inspirations. My inspiration was the women around me. Ford's inspiration came from his desire to produce an affordable car for the common man without compromising on its high quality. And finally, innovation happens only when you put your thoughts and ideated plans into action.*

12

IT'S ALL IN THE NAME

Christen your product right and it becomes a successful brand.

Knowledge from Garbage Bins

I have always been thirsty for knowledge and have quenched that thirst from all available sources. Logically, I know that gold comes from the earth and fruit from trees. In the same way, if we search well, we can get all the information that we want from the right source. I got what I sought not just from intellectuals and their books but also from the common man, the daily wagers I used to meet. Without any discrimination, I interact with everybody as I am still in the process of learning. After all, I am but a common man like them. We need to understand that everybody has something special in them. All we need is the patience to find it and learn from it.

Don't take me amiss when I say that I have learnt more from open garbage bins than from millionaires. For instance, empty food packets which have been thrown away, have helped me understand my customers by identifying the products they use in a particular area and, thus, the quantity of these products sold. By examining a garbage bin in a street, I can evaluate the health of the people who reside there.

India is a populous country and of all the business sectors, the only sector that is directly beneficial to the people is food. So, I ventured into the production of masalas in 1995, in order to cater to the needs of the masses.

Finding a Brand Name

I attribute a major part of the success of my brand to its name, one that has become synonymous with customers' lives. I wanted to choose a unique and meaningful name for my product, a name that was catchy, ineffaceable, easy to pronounce and, of course, which sounded as delicious as my masalas! I went through more than a hundred names and finally chose 'Aachi', a classical name, with a blend of the epics, history and people's lives. This name contains many unique facts.

The word 'aatchi', means 'to rule,' which in due course changed into 'aachi', denoting a woman of great knowledge, who rules her family. The Tamil epic *Silappatikaram* says that after Kovalan and Kannagi lost everything, it was the 'Aachiar' family that hosted them. In the Chettinad clan, a respectable woman by virtue of her old age, experience and care-giving attitude is addressed as 'Aachi'. If we imagine a person with that title in front of us, we would automatically feel like folding our hands before her in respect, just as we pay our respects to Mother India.

Aachi is the embodiment of wisdom and beauty. Whatever she says is right. She is an empress in cookery. So, I named my product 'Aachi'.

Aachi: A Brand Success

This name is also a positive suffix in Tamil. For example, when using the words for eating, arriving, completing in Tamil, 'Aachi' can be used as 'Sappitachi', 'Vanthachi', 'Seithachi' and so on. These are gentle, pleasant and positive words. Most Tamil people use the term 'Aachi' at least once in a conversation or at least in one sentence every day.

Today, Aachi's growth has been so wonderful that a majority of Indians use it every day in their kitchen to add spice to their culinary delights, in some form or the other.

Aachi is the mother of the Indian people. The food prepared by a mother for her child is better than any other food, because her love for the family is also mixed into it! Similarly, Aachi's fundamental principle was to provide quality and safety with motherly love in every product. The mother is identified with love. She is the foundation of hope. She is the protector and caregiver, pure and dutiful, responsible for the health of her loved ones. In the same manner, we at Aachi devoted ourselves to procuring excellent raw materials, manufacturing the best product and packing every single packet with the same motherly care.

I always like to create something new in everything I venture into, so my first innovative product in spices was the Aachi Kuzhambu Chilli Powder, a masala which can be used to make twelve different types of curries. This masala, which consisted of chillies, coriander, cumin and other spices, could be used to make both vegetarian and non-vegetarian curries, right from fish curry to egg curry! Twenty-one years ago, this twelve-in-one masala powder created quite a sensation when it was launched and was hailed as the mother of all masalas.

How Aachi Became an Instant Hit

Aachi Kuzhambu Chilli Powder came in handy for women who lost sleep worrying about what curry to make the next day. Even if they wanted to make 'karakuzhambu' (a curry with tamarind), all they needed was Aachi Kuzhambu Chilli Powder. Otherwise, they would have had to run to the shop in the morning and buy the different masalas needed to make the curry.

When at home, women cannot run to the shop each time they need something, because they would have to dress properly before stepping out. And, in case they sent a lazy husband or their child to the shop, they would have to hear their complaints. This could lead to ugly quarrels and unwanted unpleasantness in the family.

If the separate ingredients were available in the kitchen, they would have to be taken out one by one and then mixed in the right proportions to make the curry. This would need a lot of time. To avoid these issues and to make cooking easy, Aachi brought masala mixes to the kitchen, one masala to make twelve kinds of curries. So, women were able to make whatever curry they wanted, at any time. This was quite a relief for the womenfolk and it also prevented bad moods early in the day and made families a lot more peaceful!

However, the process of mixing ingredients to prepare a concoction for twelve different kinds of curries and taking it to every kitchen was not accomplished magically in a jiffy. It took a lot of time and research and, while a labour of love, was also a well-planned task. Many plans were made and had to be carefully executed. Thelma and I toiled day and night for six months to achieve this. We carefully prepared different kinds of masalas, concentrating on quality and taste, and mixed them one by one in different proportions and tested them by tasting and improving the taste step by step. We also tested them by making different kinds of curries.

Once we were satisfied with the result, we distributed the masalas to more than a hundred people and prepared charts based on those reports.

During this time, our house functioned like a mini-hotel. We created new kinds of curries and tasted everything we made. Thelma's education in home science was an added advantage. Only after getting a satisfactory report from all those who tasted the products, was each formula approved.

I must say that in the initial days, when Aachi masalas were introduced and marketed, I did not face the difficulties that I had faced with my liquid blue. Right from the beginning, Aachi won the hearts of women and their support because of its quality, taste, nutritional value, minimal preparation time, easy usage and low cost. Hence, I did not have much trouble in marketing the masalas. Within a short span, Aachi grew by leaps and bounds.

'What's in a name? A rose by any other name would smell as sweet!' goes the popular Shakespearean saying. It may be true in a literary context but not so when it comes to a brand name. A brand name is a tool for the recognition of a product by customers.

Many research studies show that if customers feel that a name is meaningful and appropriate, they remember it better, like it more, associate themselves with it and use it more frequently.

'Niveus' in Latin means 'snow white'. The brand name 'Nivea' is derived from 'Niveus'. The purity of the Nivea brand image is mirrored in the name of the company's product, skin cream.

When Jeff Bezos founded his company, he was looking for

a brand name beginning with 'A'. As he went through different names, he was attracted to the name of the largest river in the world, Amazon. His vision for the company was for it to become the biggest company in the world. The brand name stood for the large range of products that the company offered to its customers. Concurrently, the logo was also designed with a yellow arrow placed below the name, starting from the letter 'A' and pointing to the 'Z', indicating that everything from A to Z would be available on Amazon.com.

The brand name Tata (acquired from the promoter's family name, Tata) has come to stand for trust, because of its continuous accomplishment of unfailing customer satisfaction in all its businesses. Virgin, which began as the 'first experience' of its promoters, eventually built its own brand name to underscore the fresh experience that customers would enjoy. The brand Lexus, which belongs to the Japanese car maker Toyota, instantly recalls a feeling of luxury. Viagra denotes virility and vitality. All these brands have been built by virtue of their aptly positioned product profile, communication strategy and service deliveries, to be eventually known by customers for what they mean to them.

In the Korean language, 'Sam' means 'three' and 'Sung' means 'star'. 'Samsung' means 'tri-star or three stars', the three stars which represent big, numerous and powerful. The brand became an instant hit in Korea and worldwide. Customers associate the brand with its size, quality, diverse product portfolio and its powerful service back-up.

LG got its name from an abbreviation of Lucky Goldstar.

Badly conceived names bring unfortunate associations to consumers' minds. In the 1980s, United Airlines tried to transform itself into an expanded travel organization and was rebranded as Allegis. The attempt was a big failure, as people could not easily relate to it. Many could not associate the new name with the airline. Donald Trump, who has huge faith in brand-name power, is believed to have said at that time that the name sounded 'like the next world-class disease.' Soon, the airline went back to its old brand name, United Airlines.

Indian consumers do not relate to some brand names as they find their products irrelevant, even though they may be successful in other countries, because the product name does not appeal to customers. Kellogs is popular in the United States, to the extent of having a whopping 40 per cent market share in the breakfast foods category—but it has failed miserably to make inroads into the Indian market. The brand was beyond any consumer understanding. Indian consumers could not relate to the very use of breakfast cereal because our breakfast habits are so different from those in the West. Freshly prepared foods like chapatis, idli, dosa, poori, vegetables and fruits are the choicest breakfast items for Indians.

I conceptualized the brand name Aachi very carefully, with the meanings and associations of the name worked out appropriately, and the brand name was an instant success with its customers. Aachi means 'The Mother of Good Taste', convenient, ready to cook, ready to eat, of a high quality and affordable. Aachi, as a brand name, has such vivid positivity in its meaning and essence that customers have been able to clearly identify with it. Aachi has become indelible in people's minds, only to remain forever!

A clear product vision and the consequent product range creation, following customer needs and wants are the essential prerequisites for creating a big brand. A brand name must be chosen to strike the perfect note with customers. A brand needs to have a clear and understandable rationale that goes behind its creation, so that customers are able to associate with it, instantly.

Brand names that are not well conceived may kill a company; the success of a brand depends on its relevance to its target consumer needs. A thorough customer understanding, in terms of their expectations, is necessary to build a successful brand because the longevity of a brand is directly proportional to its customer expectation fulfilment.

Every attribute of the brand is a promise to the customer and if these promises are not delivered as expected, the brand could end in a big fiasco. Finally, a brand ought to continuously engage its customers by giving them tangible benefits such as excellent value and customer delight.

13

THE FOUR MS OF BUSINESS: MEN, MATERIALS, MACHINERY AND MONEY

Put men first and your business will meet with success!

Great Leaders and Their Thoughts

There are many similarities between Martin Luther King Jr and Mahatma Gandhi. King fought for the rights of black people, inspired by Gandhi's method of ahimsa, and was therefore, called 'Black Gandhi'. Like Gandhi, King was also shot dead.

Here are some of my favourite quotes from Martin Luther King Jr.

> *Love is the only force capable of transforming*
> *an enemy into a friend.*

> *Darkness cannot drive out darkness; only light can do that.*
> *Hate cannot drive out hate; only love can do that.*

We must accept finite disappointment,
but never lose infinite hope.

The time is always right to do what is right.

The Best Work Is Produced When Workers Are Happy

Generally, those who are switched off at work are easily identifiable; they go around with drooping eyes, longing to fall asleep and sporting a very tired face. There isn't much joy in those who consider their job to be a burden. Nowadays, even college students wear the same appearance as they feel the hopelessness of a bleak future looming before them.

As an entrepreneur who eventually created job opportunities for many thousands, I wanted to change this scenario. I always believed that only when the employees are happy and satisfied, can a business thrive, and I wanted to implement this rule in my company and I succeeded. My workers, who are the pillars of my success, enter the office with a big smile, while greeting one another cheerfully. I enjoy this every day, as it is a marvellous sight to see skilled men, women and their powerful machines working harmoniously. My office is a place where man meets technology.

Maintaining Hygiene in the Workplace

The hygiene inside the factory premises and the quality of products are two significant things that I can never compromise with. My vision was to provide products of a high quality to customers, so I focused on manufacturing processes to attain that level of excellence.

From my executives to workers, all of them are taught the basics of good hygiene. We instruct workers to wear specially made caps, to avoid hair falling into food products and also to wear a mask over their nose and mouth. Women do not wear anything ornamental such as flowers, bindi or glass bangles. Their nails are neatly trimmed and all mobile phones are strictly prohibited.

The same steps are followed by anyone who enters the factory. Keeping in mind the hygiene and quality of our products, visitors' watches, wallets, mobile phones, etc. are put away and kept safely in our security officer's room. As they enter the factory, they are also given a cap to cover their head in order to prevent hair from falling into products. Even I cannot escape the rule and that's the kind of consciousness my people have towards hygiene.

Quality of Raw Materials

Our raw materials, such as dal, cumin, fenugreek, pepper and so on, come loaded on trucks. Every single item is of the best quality and directly bought from farmers from various parts of India. Though great care is taken to ensure the quality of raw materials during procurement, our quality control officers also collect samples and take each item to the laboratory, packed in specially made bottles. They are thoroughly examined, approved for their quality and only then are the trucks unloaded.

Modern laboratories function inside each Aachi factory. World-class instruments, highly qualified technical researchers and skilled technologists work here.

The godown is spick and span and raw material is not stacked tightly against walls but arranged neatly on structures that leave sufficient space for air circulation, in order to preserve them hygienically.

Testing at Every Stage

All the items taken from the godown are again tested for their freshness. Let us take dal as an example: After it has been tested, it is roasted in a huge machine. Our workers ensure that the roasting machines are shining and spotless. In one single action, a thousand kilos of dal are roasted in the machine, the panel of which has a touchscreen on which the roasting temperature is entered. Within a few minutes, the whole lot is roasted evenly and sent out of the machines. Other masalas which have to be added to the dal are also roasted automatically in their respective machines at the required temperature. The people who visit my factory always exclaim how incredible it is to watch these gigantic machines roasting tonnes of masalas with one single push of a button.

All the products that are roasted in the giant machines then reach the batching area. If ten ingredients are to be mixed to make biryani masala, all the ten are roasted separately. If eight ingredients are mixed to make sambar masala, all the eight are roasted separately. Only if the ten ingredients required for the biryani masala are mixed in the exact measures, will the masala have the perfect taste. It is the same with the sambar masala, too.

Exact Ratio of Mixing

The success of Aachi masalas lies in the mixing of all the ingredients in an exact ratio and the 'secret' lies with two mothers, who are directed by Thelma. These three 'mothers' safeguard the trade secret. It is Thelma who makes the final decision if the flavour of any masala has to be altered, whether it is Gobi Manchurian masala or vathakuzhambu masala. Then, the masala is sent for scientific testing to the development department and further processes are carried out. The two women in the batching unit maintain the secrets so well that no other person knows them.

The development department decides the type of masala to be prepared, as well as its amount a day before, and the required ingredients for that masala are selected, cleaned, roasted, batched up, powdered and packed. They are packed in colourful packets starting from 8 gms to 10 kilos. The packed masalas are carefully shifted to the godown in Ayanambakkam.

In addition to factories at Ayanambakkam and Red Hills in suburban Chennai, I also established a state-of-the-art hi-tech cold grinding facility for spices at the vast State Industries Promotion Corporation of Tamil Nadu (SIPCOT) spices park in Gummidipoondi. This facility can grind spices in a way that retains their aroma for a longer shelf life. One has only to visit this factory to admire the lush green landscape with blooming colourful flowers, which extend a warm welcome to our visitors. Our trucks are systematically parked outside, completing the beautiful scene, and each one of them bears the line, 'My presence shall go before you.'

To cater to the huge demand, our factories function non-stop and one can witness this right from the entrance. On one side, the trucks unload the dried chillies and on the other side, the ground chillies are loaded to be sent out of the factory. To produce this wonderful aromatic chilli powder, top-notch modern machines and a number of people work cheerfully together.

Quality Checked Right from Unloading

Though we procure dried chillies of a high quality from various parts of India, an initial quality check is done right in the truck itself, even before unloading. The colour and the spices are tested and only when found to be excellent, are they unloaded.

The process of procuring the chillies and grinding them is very interesting. These chillies are plucked from the garden and dried in the fields. This process is done by the farmers locally. As small stones tend to get mixed up with the pure chillies, we have modern machines which remove the stones and dirt from the chillies, thereby making them clean.

Though the chillies have been dried by the farmers, some of them still have some moisture content. Such chillies cannot be ground into a fine powder easily. They also do not have a long shelf life, so these chillies which are already manually ground, are dried again in the drying machines. A single dryer in this Tech Park has the capacity to dry 5,000 kilos of chillies at a time.

Once the chillies are completely dry, the pre-cutting machines cut the chillies before powdering them. Powdering is the most important phase. If the chillies get hot or are kept exposed while grinding, they will lose their aroma. So, in order to retain the flavour, spice and aroma of the chillies, world-class modern imported machines are used. They are gigantic mill-like structures which do not generate heat while grinding. This is called cold grinding technology.

Aachi and Its Modern Machinery

I am proud to say that the Aachi factory is the only one in the whole of India that has such spectacular modern machines and the latest technology.

The ground chillies are sent to the blending machines where they are loaded onto silos for packaging. Finally, they reach the packing assembly, housed on a single floor, where the chillies are filled into millions of packets, at lightning speed. Workers carefully stack them in quantified arrays in cartons. This is how the chilli powder of Asia's No. 1 fastest growing Aachi masala is produced.

The Aachi factory in Sengundram near Chennai manufactures more than fifty food items such as pickle, ginger-garlic paste, asafoetida and snacks.

Pickles

Our pickles tickle the nostrils and touch the taste buds with their inviting smell. We produce nearly twenty types of vegetarian and non-vegetarian pickles. The quality of the final product is monitored carefully, right from the time the ingredients enter the factory.

Rice Pastes

Today's women have a hectic schedule, juggling family and career. In order to make their life easier, I tried to make their cooking simple and easy. Aachi produces and markets readymade food items in the form of pastes. More than twenty types of pastes, such as lemon rice paste, tamarind rice paste, tomato garlic paste, curry leaves rice paste, are made. The pastes only need to be mixed with hot cooked rice and, in a few moments, you have tasty dishes!

Ragi and Samba

In the old days, my grandmother would make ragi, samba and millets as part of our daily meal. Today's women know the health benefits of these items but they do not have the time to prepare them. To make their work easier and to add healthy food to every family, we have made the Aachi ragi flour, samba puttu flour, etc. Like all our other products, special attention is given to cleaning, roasting, grinding and packing. The women who work in these sections make every food product with care and discipline and the help of our machines, just as a mother would prepare food for her children in the kitchen.

These products have gained popularity among women only because of their quality and taste and we make sure that we procure fresh raw materials and produce the best products with utmost care.

Water

Health-conscious people buy purified water in bottles or cans for drinking, which has created a high demand for Aachi purified drinking water. We have a purifying unit which takes the water through seven stages. It has four micro-filters which remove every bit of bacteria present in the water. After allowing the drinking water to pass through several stages of testing, it is bottled up or canned in a hygienic way. After forty-eight hours, the water is tested in the lab and is marketed only once the results are found to be satisfactory.

Aachi's International Products

Aachi food products, which maintain international standards, are now exported to more than thirty countries. For this, a special department functions under the name of Aachi Masala Food Export in Koladi, near Chennai. This branch exports special masalas and food items to countries like the USA, Australia, Denmark and South Africa, according to the tastes of the people living there. These products are packed in attractive packets labelled with the language of the respective country. They are packed securely in a fourfold system and are ready for shipment. About 110 types of masalas and food products are manufactured in the export unit, along with readymade products such as Gulab Jamun mix, Badam mix, Jalebi mix, Rava Idli mix, Rava Upma mix, etc. Aachi's popular curry masalas and garam masalas are also made in a way that retains their fine aroma.

In one part of the factory, all the packing materials needed to pack the Aachi products are manufactured. This functions under the name 'Flora Laminates'.

There is another unit of Aachi masalas, called Blesso, in Ambattur near Chennai. Here, a variety of oil, honey, cough syrup and north and south Indian masalas are made.

Looking Back and Preserving History

The mother unit and the place where my journey began, is the laundry blue unit, which is in Padi, Thiruvalluvar Nagar, Chennai. We began our journey from a small house there, back in the 1990s, when we bottled and sold liquid blue. It was Ms Dhanalakshmi's house. She was the one who did the job of bottling the liquid blue. She had financial problems while completing the construction of the house and had rented out the house for Rs 1,000. I gave her an advance of Rs 40,000 for forty months of rent, with which she constructed a thatched roof on the top floor. She gave us the rooms on the ground floor, where, along with five other women, she poured liquid blue into bottles and packed them. That small house, which housed the beginnings of my business, stands majestically with two floors today. Ms Dhanalakshmi is still working in the Twinkle liquid blue factory cheerfully, even at the age of seventy-five, with no desire to part from our company; the only difference is that back then, she had done everything manually for a daily wage of Rs 20, but today she happily works with modern machines, receiving quite a generous salary. I admire her integrity and loyalty when she says that she will continue working until her time is up.

I have many such faithful workers who have travelled with me, sharing my success, proving that we have not just won the trust of our customers, but have also been a pioneer in winning the loyalty of our workers.

Our godown is in West Ayanambakkam, where two hundred workers are employed, with nearly a hundred transport trucks plying constantly. It is from these godowns that all the products are sent to distributors, depending on the orders placed by them. The huge, packed bundles are transported to the trucks at lightning speed on conveyor belts. These packages reach the shops through our numerous distributors, according to the needs of the customers.

Putting Man First

I find much happiness in being hospitable to people. My workers are the people who are behind my success and I find pleasure in offering lunch to them—a full meal consisting of rice, koottu, poriyal, rasam, pickle and papad, so that they don't have to carry lunch to my factories. But even this story has a background. One day, after my meeting with the factory authorities, I was heading to the dining hall with my workers. Since I pay attention to everything that happens around me, to my surprise I found a woman eating stale rice porridge. This moved me to tears. I felt that my workers should be given fresh food. Immediately, I convened a meeting with my factory officials and asked them to organize hygienic, tasty and fresh food for all our workers. From that day on, food is served to all workers, free of cost, in all our factories.

To help those in need is like helping God himself! Put a man first in your business, over all the other essentials such as material, machinery and money, and you will be sure to meet success.

This chapter says a great deal about the pains I have taken to ensure every step of Aachi's progress in food processing. People are the backbone of the business and they need to be taken care of well, and provided with the right opportunities and environment to work in.

I dislike the hierarchical structure of managers. I think a multirung hierarchy is taxing for an organization. Managers are a significant part of a big overhead. In many organizations, the weight of managers is heavy. For example, for 5,000 employees in manager-heavy organizations, there could be 500 managers in a 1:10 ratio. First, such a large workforce of managers pulls down performance. Second, the huge hierarchical structure could delay decisions, as issues may have to pass through various levels of the hierarchy before arriving at solutions. So, more levels would mean more layers of decision-making and, consequently, delayed approvals. Third, a big hierarchical structure involves greater expenditure for the organization, which may result in higher prices of products.

There is no hierarchy in the manpower structure of all the Aachi group of companies. At Aachi, we have people from very simple backgrounds who manage each business. The members of each team in every factory are trained so well that a very lean, mean and fit structure in the manufacturing process renders every product cost-efficient and, hence, affordable to the customer.

Teamwork, product quality, process efficiency and cost consciousness are the four key aspects that I emphasize on. If you look carefully at these four aspects, you can see that they clearly relate to men, materials, machinery and money.

When it comes to teamwork in the Aachi group of companies, one can see people working in the factories with a high level of commitment. Each factory has very little supervisory and managerial staff and people work with their own personal efforts to achieve results.

I have read about the world's largest tomato processing company in Woodland, California, called Morning Star where people have been trained to manage themselves! The company believes in neither designations nor promotions. The employees manage the entire manufacturing process by perfect coordination among themselves. Even appraisals are inter-departmental and compensations are peer-based. Each employee understands their role in ensuring the company's profitable operations and they are careful about quality processing and timely deliveries to customers like supermarkets and bulk buyers. Over the past twenty years, Morning Star has achieved a double-digit growth with the efficient support of its three large manufacturing units. At Morning Star, people are motivated by their own mission and commitment and not by any manager. Employees at Morning Star sign an agreement with the colleagues who are affected by their work, to help themselves achieve better results through what is called a Colleague Letter of Understanding (CLOU, pronounced 'clue'), which is a sort of operating plan often containing numerous self-developed metrics for fulfilling each one's mission. Aachi's employees are quite similar. They work with their own personal mission to achieve results, but with an unwritten agreement for passionate involvement in their job! Since Aachi cares for its employees with its unmatched welfare measures such as free lunch, free medical aid, etc., it adds to the motivation among employees to be self-performers.

Quality is my byword in business. I am always keen to buy the right quality of raw materials. I personally supervise raw material procurement in order to ensure quality output. Quality consciousness is driven top-down in every manufacturing unit of Aachi so that each employee knows that there can be no compromise on quality. My quest and drive for quality begin from the environment. I visit my factories often. My habit is to get down from the car right at the entrance, walk right around the factory and check for any littering or dumping in the open areas. If I find anything, I do not hesitate to pick it up myself and I sensitize everyone about upkeep and tidiness. I inspect a product at every step in the process, personally checking its quality and advising employees on the need to always be quality-focused. My factory visit does not end without going into every unit's quality testing centre, where I spend quality time with the laboratory technicians and quality experts, discussing further improvements. Internal training on quality is a way of life in every Aachi unit, where one can always find a devoted resource for such interventions and coaching on quality parameters to follow.

I never hesitate to invest in the best machinery available for processing. All Aachi units are equipped with the right machinery. Even in the initial days, when machines were not available for some specific operations, I encouraged manufacturers to customize machinery for us. Before my sons Ashwin and Abhishek entered the business, I did my own research to find the right machinery. Both my sons now focus on acquiring state-of-the-art machinery for quality processing. The cold grinding facility at Gummidipoondi stands testimony to the fact that Aachi does not leave any stone unturned to establish quality infrastructure and machinery for grinding masalas and spices. This technology, which is new to India, has been procured from countries such as Japan and Germany. The grinding process reduces the material to millions of tiny particles that hit against each other at high velocity repeatedly and in such a way that the process does not generate any heat at all, so that the aroma is retained. The dry, cold and inert atmosphere in the grinding chamber ensures that there is no thermal reaction with the material and reduces any loss of quality during processing.

My philosophy of business growth is to take one step at a time. I believe in the Chinese proverb that says, 'It is better to take many small steps in the right direction than to make a great leap forward only to stumble backwards.' I have the innate inclination to recognize when and how to expand capacities; I begin my work on additional capacity installation or on a new factory as soon as an old unit crosses more than half of its installed capacity. I understand timelines and gear up my people to work on additional capacities sufficiently in advance so that Aachi customers are never disappointed.

Take care of your people and they will take care of your business; when they are self-motivated, they perform at their best. Remember that a hygienic work environment must be a way of life and it should be non-negotiable in food processing. Drive the consciousness of quality in everything you do and invest in the right machinery to ensure the best output. Commit to continuous process improvement; each improvement should result in cost savings, which can be passed on to customers. As you grow your business, make sure that you take just one just step at a time.

14

ENTREPRENEURS WON'T FAIL IF THEY REALIZE THEIR SPECIAL SOCIAL PURPOSE

Know your purpose as a businessman!
How do we stay healthy? By eating what nature has provided for us, right? Man has been eating what nature provides and has remained healthy by doing so. Man used to work hard in the fields and earn his bread and livelihood by the sweat of his brow. A figurative expression is found in the Bible in Genesis, where God punished Adam for eating the forbidden fruit in the Garden of Eden, saying, 'In the sweat of thy face shalt thou eat bread.' God said that Man would have to work hard for his bread. Man toiled and was very healthy.

The Bhagavad Gita says that the foods that promote life, vitality, strength, health, happiness and satisfaction, and are succulent, juicy, nourishing and pleasing to the heart, are dear to us. An authorized commentary says: 'To those who are situated in sattvaguna, the mode of goodness, foods that are of the nature of sattva or goodness, such as milk, fruits, grains and vegetables, are very dear. Such foods promote long life, invigorating the body and elevating the mind in its function of intelligence.' Today's new food habits have come from so-called modern thinking, with the man adopting unhealthy eating habits with little self-control. Stale, tasteless, rancid and putrid food is dear only to the ignorant, according to the Gita. Man has become ignorant of healthy food habits and this situation needs to change.

Emphasis on Research and Development

One fundamental reason behind the success of Aachi Masala Food Products is its continuous emphasis on research and development (R&D). The Aachi R&D department has a team of qualified food technologists and scientists who work on product development tirelessly. They work to fulfil the needs of people and this department functions in an excellent manner with its experienced researchers. Here, ultra-modern technical instruments are used. 'Day by day, people's needs, desires and expectations are changing. So, we must act according to these changes and cater to the needs of the people,' is the principle on which the Aachi R&D functions.

Knowing well that changes alone can encourage a man and make him relish and enjoy life, we keenly observe the Indian health scenario, especially the changes within it. Currently, India is on its way to become the 'capital city of diabetic people'. Previously, countries like the US and the UK were leading in the number of obese people, but today in India, there has been a rapid increase in the number of obese people. It is the same with cardiac patients, too.

Research on People's Health

The employees in this department always ask questions like: 'At what age do these diseases attack a man? Which category of people gets affected? Which is greater, the number of male heart patients or female heart patients? What are the reasons behind these kinds of diseases?' In the early days, diabetes, heart disease, obesity, etc., afflicted people only after a particular age. Now, even youngsters have become victims of these diseases. Similarly, school students, college students and pregnant women used to be healthy, dynamic and energetic, whereas today even young girls, teenagers and pregnant women are found to be anaemic. The reason for this is that they do not have a balanced diet, which lowers their immunity. Similarly, young boys and old people are also easily affected by these conditions. Keeping all these things in mind, the R&D department works with a focused social consciousness and creates new food items that improve the immune system, speed up healing and help prevent diseases. They do this through thorough research.

Indians are at par with the rest of the world in appreciating and relishing good food. India has now become a melting pot for all kinds of food from all over the world. People get various recipes from the Internet and make them in their kitchen. The R&D department caters to the needs of these people.

A healthy India is our fundamental goal. So, we pay full attention not only to taste but also to the quality of the product and health of the consumers. For this purpose, the R&D department carefully collects health-related statistics of the world and compares them to our own. The eyes and ears of our R&D department are always open. We always warmly welcome the opinions and ideas of customers, consumers, small shopkeepers, common people, doctors and researchers.

Every customer rightfully expects fresh food products from Aachi, the same way a child expects this from his own mother. We fulfil their expectations with taste, quality and health. Our R&D department functions purely for the sake of the people. That is how we have developed an inseparable bond with Indian families.

Salient Features of the R&D Department

- Identifying people's daily needs;
- Planning and creating food items desired by people;
- Continually monitoring and collecting statistics on India's health;
- Taking measures accordingly to improve general health conditions through food;
- Introducing new food items;
- Recognizing the food needs of people of all ages;
- Creating favourite food products for all age groups;
- Observing the financial and living conditions of people and prioritizing food products according to that;
- Reducing the time spent in the kitchen by making food items that can be cooked quickly;
- Foreseeing changes in the health of the people in the next five to ten years through discussions with experts from the medical field and bringing necessary alterations in the food;
- Maintaining a high standard to ensure that consumers of Aachi food products are healthy;
- Innovating high-quality and tasty products at an affordable price.

For example, the Gulab Jamun mix is made in line with all the following ideas: It should not consume a lot of oil; it should be very soft; it should render itself in texture to be made into small balls; it should melt in the mouth; it should have an excellent flavour and colour; it should be possible to cut it easily with a spoon but it should not break; it should have a long shelf life; it should make the consumer want more.

Tasters to Keep the Taste Tasty

Like coffee and tea makers who employ tasters for their products through whom the taste is measured, we also do the same. There is a high demand for such tasters at an international level and they are guarded like treasures by the companies. All our food products are tasted by these tasters. Our tasters are very health-conscious and keep their bodies and minds fresh by performing physical and breathing exercises every day. They maintain a strict diet and they have absolutely no bad habits like alcoholism, smoking, chewing tobacco or betel leaves. Though their physical condition is generally good, sometimes they might catch a cold or fall sick. At such times, they are not allowed to carry out any tasting. Only those who are fully healthy are employed.

The R&D department also follows certain rules for tasting. The tasters can taste the products only at a particular time and under certain conditions. They cannot taste food when they are famished because everything would be very tasty for them. Similarly, if they taste when their stomachs are full, they could underestimate the taste. Hence, taking into account their daily food intake, food habits, time of eating, etc., they are given the job of tasting.

All operations of the Aachi R&D department are scientific.

A taste chart has been prepared, based on scientific research. It asks, what will a food product taste like, initially? What will it taste like after some time? How long will the taste last?

Food products are put through surveys and opinion polls, where target customers are made to identify their taste, quality, flavour and colour. Based on the reports, new products are developed. Most importantly, products are monitored to be at a level which can improve the consumer's health. In this manner, many new products have been introduced. The Aachi R&D department, which has prepared two hundred food products, is preparing to introduce fifty more in the next few years.

The Tongue and How It Functions

The tongue is the most important organ of taste; it is always curious and can identify different tastes. The tongue is slightly rough because of the presence of the papillae, which have thousands of taste buds at the tip. Taste buds are present on the upper and lower part of the tongue, inside the cheeks and the lips. Nearly eighteen receptacles are present in each taste bud and they send the taste signal to the brain. These taste buds and papillae can be seen through a magnifying glass. Surprisingly, some people have more taste buds and some others may have fewer.

When the eye sees food, the brain becomes interested in finding out how it tastes and, thus, the urge to eat is kindled. As a result, saliva is produced automatically. This saliva is essential to feel the taste and help in digestion. It helps the food to be ground, ingested, pushed in and digested easily. Only when the mouth is wet with saliva can the taste of food be fully relished.

When we have fever, the secretion of saliva is reduced and,

hence, our tongue becomes dry. Then, exact tastes cannot be identified. That's why sick people cannot taste anything and say that they are not interested in eating.

Interestingly, the lifespan of taste buds is just ten days. The old ones are replaced by new ones in a cyclical process. When we have something very hot, the tongue gets scalded and the taste buds stop functioning temporarily. But, the next day, they are created anew and regain their ability to taste.

Children have more taste buds than adults, which is why they are able to taste sweetness, heat and bitterness more distinctly. However, newborn babies have very few taste buds.

The tongue is used not only to taste and eat food but also to talk; it is essential for human communication. If not for the tongue, many of our languages would not have originated. The tongue has the ability to function differently while eating and talking. When a person talks, the tongue gently folds and moves but while eating its movements become sharp because it has to chew, grind and help in swallowing.

As an age-old saying goes, a tongue can speak whatever it wants to because it has no nerves, but that's just a myth. The tongue has a supply of nerves but it does not have a bone. Even a person's illness and lack of nutrients can be detected by observing his tongue. I can identify anaemia and Vitamin B deficiency just by looking at a person's tongue.

Surprisingly, 15 per cent of the people in the world do not have the ability to taste. This is caused by the deficiency of zinc and Vitamin B12. We are making Aachi food products especially for these people, taking into account their inability to taste food. We pack food products attractively to motivate people to taste them. Even those who have a lowered ability of taste are enticed to taste the food and buy our products. Eventually, in this way, they are able to eat well.

Indians were the pioneers of making masalas. No one can resist the aroma of spices like clove, cinnamon, cardamom, etc., which kindle a person's hunger. We add them to all our products. Hence, through food, we improve the tasting ability of people. Also, we rectify the nutrient deficiency of people in order to improve their health.

My interest in science and my thirst to know about taste and the special functions of the tongue is another one of the major reasons for providing quality food products to my consumers who, in turn, shower praise on them.

'Healthy India', expressed in Tamil as 'Arokia India', is a vision I nurture from the perspective of social responsibility. My desire is not only to provide healthy food to Aachi's customers but also to inculcate the habit of healthy eating among them. For this reason, I have set up a state-of-the-art food-testing laboratory called Scientific Food Testing Services (SFTS) in Chennai. We established SFTS in 2014. Food safety and quality are fundamental for addressing health concerns in our country. Food safety and quality have become areas of great priority and necessity for stakeholders in the food industry such as consumers, retailers, manufacturers and food business operators. SFTS has more than sixty experienced food technologists and scientists who strive hard every day to provide quality food testing services.

Changing global patterns of food production, international trade, technology, public expectations from health and many other factors necessitate the delivery of quality food for all. We are committed to provide testing and analytical support services and end-to-end quality assurance through our SFTS, a laboratory equipped with modern instruments and equipment for food testing. Our lofty mission is to provide quality food products to society at all levels through scientific and technology-driven processes to meet national and international standards of food safety and quality. Instrumental analysis, food composition analysis, microbiological food testing and water testing are the key services SFTS offers. The key role that SFTS plays today is to support the scientific validation of nutritional products in addition to conducting nationwide nutrition surveys and development of analytical assistance and services for ensuring food safety and quality. In addition to that, SFTS supports manufacturers and other stakeholders of the food sector in the process of complying with safety guidelines and standards while providing for the nutrition and nutrition related needs of the country. SFTS is duly accredited by the National Accreditation Board for Testing and Calibration Laboratories (NABL), which is a constituent board of the Quality Council of India.

Aachi owes its business success to 'providing the common man with safe and quality food products at affordable prices'. Many food manufacturers and food processors, who avail of the services of SFTS, are able to ensure the supply of safe and quality food to the masses. My vision is to set up many such scientific food testing centres all across India in the days to come, so that the whole country can benefit from food safety and quality.

I could easily have focused only on building our masala food products processing business, where it is enough for each manufacturing unit have an R&D department. But, it is not enough to perform mandatory quality compliances within the factory; I also have a larger social concern that needed to be addressed. I went that extra mile to set up a scientific food testing facility, investing a huge amount of capital. My concern is for the health of the people of India so that the entire country can become a healthy nation. Creating a healthy India would ultimately lead to creating a wealthy India. If we eat healthy food, we can contribute tirelessly towards the growth of our country's economy.

Identify and embed a social concern or cause to address through your business. Try to conceptualize a detailed plan for addressing the cause. Work on the solutions along with people who have the experience and expertise to help you deliver your action plan. Meanwhile, seek to collaborate with available resources in the area of your business operations, to address the identified social concern. Build the required support system and the infrastructure to make sure the benefits reach the correct people. Finally, remember that when you go the extra mile to address social concerns, your business will flourish by itself!

15

ALWAYS MAINTAIN A POSITIVE ATTITUDE

Why lose heart when you fail?

Walt Disney once said, 'Many are under the impression that I have a Midas touch and that whatever I touch would turn out to be successful. But, in reality, many times I had taken wrong decisions and failed pathetically. Yet, since I was persistent in making efforts, I have come out of those failures before they could be known. Like me, if you too keep attempting, you too can become an achiever.'

Some of his quotes are extremely useful for people like us. Disney also said, 'When you fail, you may not know its value. But later, you realize that this failure, which has made you fall, is the world's greatest gift.' This thought applies to me also. So, do not lose heart. Try again and you will succeed.

Convincing Others through Your Passion

When I expressed my desire to start a business to the members of my family, there was a lot of fear and doubt about whether I would succeed. That fear was quite natural, since I had been employed, with an assured monthly remuneration. The members of my family, especially my in-laws and also my wife, were worried about how I would run my business successfully. The business needed investment of time, effort and money. Little did they know, at that time, that I would put my heart and soul into it. On first hearing about it, a few members of my family insisted that I go back to a good job. Since I was determined to start my own business, they finally came around to accept my passion. My father-in-law, who is good at cooking, even offered flavour-, taste- and quality-related suggestions for masalas. In the initial days, when Thelma and I used to shuttle between the liquid blue company and Aachi, my mother-in-law helped us to manage the former and my father-in-law the latter. My passionate focus on my business was so infectious that all the members of my family were drawn in.

In the initial days of struggle, my business did not see any success. There were no profits and expenses kept mounting. Though the sales volumes were growing, they were less than what they should have been. The FMCG business is a game of volumes. The moment you achieve good volumes, your ratio of operating expenses to turnover becomes healthy. So, I was focusing on higher volumes of sale with an increased penetration into smaller markets to achieve maximum distribution of my products. I had to extend credit to my distributors who in turn gave credit to the retailers. This vicious cycle rendered a big cash crunch in the business. While struggling, my mother-in-law and my wife did not lose confidence in me instead they encouraged and strengthened me to move forward. They had complete trust in me, confident I would succeed. They often said that they liked my courage, self-confidence, fighting spirit, tireless work and positive attitude!

When I rented a huge place in Padi, Chennai for the business, I had to do a lot of construction there. When my mother-in-law saw that, she was a little apprehensive and said that a smaller place would have been sufficient. Within the next few months, the business started to flourish. When it was doing considerably well, I planned to double the production. Again, she was afraid that by doing so, we would be storing more than selling, but within two months, the demand for Aachi masala products increased to such a great extent that everything we had made was sent to the shops. She then came to me and said that I certainly had a gift of forecasting the ups and downs of business and that whatever I said definitely proved to be correct. She also said that I had inspired her to start thinking positively.

Facing Calamities and Catastrophes Head-on

Around 1995, there was a flood in Chennai; in those days, whenever the walls of the Ambattur Lake breached, Anna Nagar was flooded. One day, the breaching of the Ayanambakkam Lake resulted in floods which waterlogged our factory, with the water reaching up to hip level. There was heavy damage which resulted in a big loss. Tonnes of coriander seeds, cumin seeds, pepper, etc., were washed away and expensive machines were damaged. The factory was submerged in water for a month. Every day, I would go there and remove everything, wading through waist-deep water. I repaired the machines and brought them back to order. Everybody was worried about the future; I told them that we should have built the factory on a raised foundation as the lake was very close to our factory, so it was our mistake. I thought positively and realized our mistake and was determined to rectify it in future. Today, I feel that this positive thinking has taken me very far.

Teaching Others to Use Failure as a Stepping Stone to Success

Experience has been my best teacher. When Ashwin and Abishek began to get involved in the business after completing their education, I gave them the freedom to make their own decisions. My intention was to give them the opportunity to learn from experience and mistakes. The sales of Aachi masalas rose to such a level that our machines became insufficient for producing the needed quantity. So, as part of the expansion plan, we had to buy a few new machines. I knew that they would be available abroad and I asked my sons to source them. Both my sons did their homework and went to South Korea to buy machines of a high standard, worth almost sixty lakhs of rupees.

The machines arrived and were installed. But they did not operate as well as they should have. My sons were dejected and thought that they had failed in their first attempt to source proper machinery for the business. But, they did not give up. After a year, the machines started operating well and helping in the production. Within that one year, my older son Ashwin had disassembled the machines, discovered the technical method of operating them and made them work. He used his technical knowledge to get the better of the situation.

Such experiences happened quite often and my sons were ready to take their plunge into making business a full-time part of their life. Later, Ashwin bought machines worth several crores of rupees and has developed them further. Now, all the machines are working well, beyond expectations. We have to realize that failures ought to be considered as new experiences. Both my sons have undertaken projects worth crores of rupees and now they execute them successfully. Failures have helped all of us realize our true potential. When we scale the heights of success, these failures are the trails of experience and learning that we leave behind us, that remind us of the path we traversed and help us not to repeat mistakes.

I always enjoy my work, irrespective of the different situations I may find myself in. I find a lot of satisfaction in spending time at my factories and workplace. When you enjoy your work, you don't have to drag your feet to attend to your duties. I find enjoyment in facing tough situations and even failures. I overcome them with my relentless efforts. If you enjoy what you do, you will excel and delight in what you do. That's the key mantra of success.

Balancing Work and Family

While I enjoy working, I also enjoy the company of my family. One needs to strike a perfect balance between one's personal and professional life. On weekends, I enjoy going out with my family and, quite often, eating out as well. My sons, when they were younger, enjoyed such days—we would go, when we went by motorcycle, and ate on the Chennai beaches or in popular shopping areas. Such a balance helped me remain positive. Once, my mother-in-law convinced me to go to Kodaikanal with the family. I went but, even after getting there, I spent a lot of time observing how my products were placed in the hill station. So, I got up early in the morning and visited the market, full of small shopkeepers and small-scale businesses. I observed the kinds of food items that were sold in those shops. I could see, from the stocks, what the sales of Aachi products were like, what people said about them and so on. That was when I realized that my business and I had become inseparable; I grasped what true ownership meant.

My journey through life has changed me in beautiful ways. Every day has brought me something useful and my failures have taught me more than my successes have. Today, I speak on a lot of spiritual matters and on matters of social concern.

Social Concerns: Helping the Poor

Helping others has always been a part of my life. Even when we were facing continuous failures and loss, I would bring home the money collected from distributors and stack the currencies and give the coins to Thelma, who would keep them separately. When the poor approached us for help, Thelma would take out these coins to give them. We never asked them to repay the debt because I saw that they needed food, which was important to understand. Today, this desire to help has become stronger, by the grace of God. Even when you go through challenging times, you must find every available resource to help the needy around you. These acts of charity will keep you in a happy and positive frame of mind.

Many who succeed in business, miserably fail in their personal life. But the reason behind my success in business is the absence of failure in my personal life. It is important for everyone to succeed in their personal life because it will pave the way to success in everything else. Every failure and challenging situation will become insignificant if you approach it with a positive mind.

Failure and success are two sides of the coin of life. So, if you want to avoid failure, you will have to do the same with success, too. Failure is more powerful than success. While success makes you smile, failure makes you think. Similarly, face criticism boldly because that alone will strengthen you and make you a successful person.

Whenever problems crop up, confront them and tackle them. Sometimes, problems wear a threatening mask, but they always come to you carrying good opportunities. When you approach problems without anxiety, you will be able to recognize the opportunity and embrace it. The opportunity is the positive side of the problem!

People around me often say that positivity is writ large on my face. My son Ashwin says, 'It was only much later in my life, say in the post-teenage years, that I came to know that Dad had faced a lot of hardships in his business. Since we always looked up to him as our hero, we could never sense even a minuscule part of his difficulties. Our parents brought us up in such a way that Abishek and I did not know about the difficulties they went through in their journey. When a person is burdened by debt or problems in his business, his appearance, manner of speaking, actions and body language can expose his tough situation. But Dad was always positive. He ensured that nobody could sense that he was in a challenging situation, from his appearance, expressions or actions. He always dressed elegantly in a corporate style. His expressions are always devoid of frustration and dejection. So, we could never realize that he was in any difficulty at any time. Dad's positivity rubbed off on all of us in the family, which today helps us tide over difficult situations, whether in our personal or professional lives.'

It is difficult to constantly maintain an attitude of happiness and joy at the workplace, especially in the midst of challenging situations. I am an emissary of positive feelings in any situation. Even when I discipline anyone for a misdeed or misdemeanor,

I do it in such a way that the person remembers it as a lesson. Once I enter my office, my full concentration centres around my work and all other worries are left behind. As you enter any of the Aachi offices, at the entrance where you leave your shoes, you find the words: 'Leave your footwear along with hatred behind!'

Amitabh Bachchan had many setbacks in life. But he nurtured a positive frame of mind and overcame his failures. He was badly injured while shooting for the film *Coolie*, but he bounced back with resilience. He had a big financial setback following the collapse of his company, Amitabh Bachchan Corporation Ltd (ABCL) in the late 1990s. His persistence to perform with a positive mind brought him back to the limelight. When he got the opportunity to anchor the *Kaun Banega Crorepati* game show, many wondered how a 70mm film hero could accept a role on the small screen—but he made the show popular with his charismatic appearance and performance. He brought great popularity to it across the country and, after that, his financial success is history. His positivity negated all criticism. Today, he stands tall, pun intended! Positivity gives the power to be resilient and attain success.

When I was working as a senior salesperson in Godrej Soaps, sales trainees would often be deputed to me for training. In 1981, as I was guiding sales trainees on their first training stint, I took them along with me to the market to redistribute the consumer products of the company, such as Cinthol soap and other items. As we walked through the market, the distributor's salespeople also came along with ready stocks on two tricycles. We entered a grocery shop with the specific objective of selling a blue detergent soap named Trilo. We could see an array of Trilo soaps on the shelves, along with other brands. One of the trainees told me that the store already had a lot of stock and the shopkeeper would not buy any more. I quietly challenged him, saying that I would sell a respectable number of cartons of Trilo to the shopkeeper. I opened the conversation, greeting the owner in a very friendly manner. With a pre-concluded guess, I told the shopkeeper that he had exhausted all the stocks we had given him earlier and the only remaining ones were on the shelves. My conclusion, following my experiential guess, was that there were no stocks in storage. The shopkeeper readily agreed with me, as he knew his stocks like the back of his hand. Since he had no more stocks in storage, I sold him ten cartons of seventy-two soaps each. While the trainee saw the stocks on the shelves and concluded that we might not sell the detergent to the retailer, I saw an opportunity the other way round. I literally 'pushed' the product on to the shopkeeper's shelves so that no competing brand could stay there. That day, my trainees learned to look at sale and stock situations differently!

From my experience, a clear focus on the task and its objectives helps you tide over ups and downs. No deviation from the focus should be allowed.

Always view things with a positive frame of mind and it will help you look at problems differently. A positive attitude can also help you to see different solutions.

Carefully balance your personal and professional life. A good work–life balance helps you perform well. If your family supports and helps you, then you have a worry-free mind that can focus on the business.

Try and change negative people into positive individuals, and if you are not able to do so, move away from them. The company of those who harbour or express negative thoughts may be detrimental to your spirit of positivity.

A constant focus on your task also focuses your efforts towards the achievement of success. Be positive in your mind and your thoughts, words and deeds will automatically become positive as well. When calamities strike, focus on solutions to get over them, rather than brooding over them. Failures are an integral part of any business. If you have not failed, you have not had the right business experience. Do not close your mind from helping others even when you are in challenging circumstances. Use the available resources to help those in need and this will bring you the greatest satisfaction. Every failure is a stepping stone of learning and experience to reach your ultimate goal!

16

CATCHING A TIGER BY THE TAIL

Success, like a butterfly, is as difficult to grasp as holding a tiger by the tail. Yet, when you finally achieve it, you enjoy it.

Mother Teresa and Compassion

When Mother Teresa was made a saint by the Catholic Church, what were your thoughts, especially about her life of compassion?

John F. Kennedy's picture adorns many homes in India, next to photos of Gandhiji and Pandit Nehru. Kennedy, one of the most famous presidents of the USA, once came to Kolkata to meet Mother Teresa. She, as usual, was engrossed in cleaning the lepers and applying medicines on their sores. Kennedy respectfully went up to greet her by shaking hands with her but she hesitated, since her hands were stained with pus and blood. Hesitantly, she said, 'Please forgive me; I have not washed my hands yet.' 'Mother!' Kennedy replied, 'I consider it a great privilege to shake your sacred hands which are stained by service!'

On 26 January 1962, impressively dressed dignitaries were seated on stage when Mother Teresa walked up in her simple clothes. Moved by her simplicity, Vijaya Lakshmi Pandit turned to Prime Minister Jawaharlal Nehru with tears in her eyes. Nehru, too, was deeply touched. President Rajendra Prasad honoured Mother Teresa with the Padma Shri. She was the first foreigner to receive this honour.

In 1964, the Christians' Conference was held in Mumbai. It was presided over by President Dr S. Radhakrishnan, in the august presence of Pope John Paul II (Pope VI). Delighted by Mother's services, he presented her with his white Lincoln Continental car. It was a gesture of goodwill for Mother's services.

Everyone thought that Mother Teresa would not be seen walking on the streets after that and would travel by her luxury car. But, within six hours, she did something that astonished everyone. She auctioned the car for a huge sum of money and built a massive hospital for lepers with that money. This benefitted more than four lakh lepers. She did not rest on her laurels. Her service never ceased.

Sainthood must have been thrilled to embrace her!

Everything in the world has been created with a purpose, to serve as an example and a lesson for all human beings, even small beings like the ant, or huge ones like the elephant and even soil and trees! We cannot learn these lessons from our teachers or parents or anybody else. It is difficult to learn these things even from experience.

Yet, some people grasp this knowledge through their profound thinking, and then they share their experience with others. I think I belong to this set of people.

Business Is Like a Butterfly

In a park inside a resort in Andhra Pradesh, nestled among

lush green pastures in Kumili, Thelma and I were seated one evening, enjoying the panoramic sight of clouds brushing against the mountaintops. Colourful butterflies dotted the entire area, fluttering their wings gaily.

I was keenly observing them and asked Thelma, 'Which flower looks the most beautiful to you?' She said with a smile, 'Those butterflies…,' pointing at a swarm of butterflies crowding around a flower.

I immediately appreciated what she had observed and patted her on the shoulder. I couldn't help saying, 'Like a butterfly, you too have fascinated an entire community of youngsters. Many are in awe of your ideas, efficiency and success in the same way as the beauty and colours of these butterflies charm people.'

I continued, 'I am also like this butterfly. Today, many are amazed to see me flying with the colours of success. Just like a butterfly which used to be a caterpillar and had to transition through being a pupa, I went through a phase when I had to shut myself in a shell and struggle for success. Truly, a butterfly is a classic example of my life.'

The female butterfly lays eggs which are too small to be noticed by the human eye. Like these eggs, I was also an insignificant person in society, hardly noticed by anyone. The mother butterfly is intelligent. Realizing that the caterpillar needs food, she lays her eggs on healthy, edible leaves. My mother, like the mother butterfly, was intelligent, took care of me and provided me with all that I required till I graduated from college.

Like the caterpillars coming out of the safety of the eggs, I left the safety of my job, to start my own business. Some people looked down on me, like they look down on a caterpillar. They abandoned me and treated me with disdain.

From its abdomen, the caterpillar ejects a thin silky threadlike strand and builds a strong cocoon around itself for safety, then confines itself inside the cocoon. That's when we call it a larva. This phase lasts for several days. Similarly, I did not mingle with society and confined myself inside a cocoon of hard labour. According to entomology, the caterpillar lies unmoving within the pupa, just to strengthen its exoskeleton. At this time, nobody can see any life inside the pupa. I also remained silent for a long time, only to strengthen myself. I had this kind of a life for several years, when I restricted myself to a shell, disconnected from outsiders, kith and kin. My only actions were related to my business. Some people, who could not understand this stage of my life, might have even imagined that I was ruined. But, during that time, I was focusing on all my potential, like in a meditative stage.

In the next phase, the butterfly undergoes a wonderful metamorphosis. Its appearance changes dramatically, both inside and outside. The wings of the butterfly, which are its most beautiful parts, start growing in this phase and they help the butterfly to fly, flaunting its beautiful colours. The fourth phase was colourful in my life too, as the wings of success grew. Today, to everyone's amazement, I fly, flaunting my skills in the business world, just like the butterfly.

Many youngsters admire thus stage of my life. I would like to tell them that the larva phase of life was terribly agonizing for me. It was full of pain, failures and shame.

I went through the many humiliations that an average man goes through when he wants to start his own business. But, I enjoyed my failures, and now, I am a fully grown butterfly and enjoy tasting the honey of success.

Butterflies are one of the best creations of God. They are not only beautiful, but they also carry lessons for life. They are good examples for me and they will be good examples for you too.

Success brings not just a vicious cycle but also a cycle of virtue.

Catching a Tiger by the Tail

A familiar phrase in Tamil, 'like catching the tail of a tiger…', comes to our mind the minute we see a tiger.

When we see a tiger, we think that such a phrase is sheer nonsense, as the very sight of a tiger is intimidating, and catching its tail is impossible. So, we put the thought out of our mind, saying that it is meaningless.

But, I did catch the tail of a tiger. I have been pulled by it, wounded by it, wrestled with it, day and night. It has tried to chase me and has scared me. It has pushed me down and tried to devour me. Yet, I did not let go of its tail and eventually succeeded in sitting astride it successfully.

Are you surprised by this statement? Remember that 'catching the tail of a tiger' is a principle of life. It is the formula for the success of a common man.

A tiger's tail is 3-4 feet long, which makes it easy to catch. Once you catch the tail, you must hold on to it with all your might, day and night, otherwise, it could throw you off. If you let go of the tiger's tail after catching it, it will be your end!

The footprints of a tiger are as unique as the palm prints of human beings. They differ from tiger to tiger. Using their sharp and strong claws, tigers hunt their prey. India has the largest number of tigers in the world and they are our national animal.

I have been known as a successful businessman since 2000. Holding on to the tail of a tiger called success, I have suffered and struggled a lot. For ten years, the struggle was so intense that

I faced great failures. I wrestled with those failures determinedly, never letting go of the tail, no matter what happened. A tiger is very strong, but I fought it wisely and carefully, so that its cruel and sharp claws could not inflict any failures on me.

A tiger can run at the speed of forty miles per hour. Many people assumed that I would be dragged along and destroyed by it, but I managed to keep up. Many people saw the sharp claws and teeth of the tiger and asked me to run away from it, but I persevered! I never let go of the tiger's tail. I held on to it while I struggled to learn the secret of taming the tiger and winning against it. Of course, on a few occasions, I fell, unable to withstand it; yet, I learnt how it had made me fall and learnt to sustain myself without falling again, no matter how hard it pulled at me or tried to pin me down. I held on to the tiger of success, succeeded in the business and managed to sit astride it.

My journey on the tiger of success has been continuing since 2000. Holding on to success is as important as achieving it; you cannot rest on a bed of roses. I sit on the heroic tiger of success and I make a calculated and balanced analysis of its threats, roars, jumps and power; otherwise, I can be thrown off. Only when I work untiringly and keep up with the times, can I fight competition in the marketplace. If I keep my eyes on the welfare of my people, then this tiger of success will always remain under my control and carry me forward. So, don't think that I, having touched the peak of success in food products, am sitting back happily. Now, astride the tiger, I am more alert than ever!

A successful entrepreneur's life is like that of a butterfly, going through many transformations before becoming what it is. The experience of an entrepreneur can be compared to a roller coaster ride, especially in the start-up stages, when you struggle hard to gain the required momentum, and your life may go through different kinds of turmoil. Often, the struggle is to make both ends meet and find money just to set up the business. In the FMCG business, it is a big challenge to gain product acceptance with customers. When you gain consumer acceptance by expensive means like free sampling and promotions, it becomes a bigger challenge to support the shopkeepers to stock the items and sustain consumer interest. Retail shopkeepers often try to sell only the products from multinational companies, because they find them easy to sell. So, it becomes a game of offering greater margins to the retailers to motivate them to stock the products. Even if you gain both retailer and consumer confidence with hard work, credit lines are a big worry. Everyone in the supply chain, distributors and retail shopkeepers alike, ask for a month's credit and often it does not end within that time frame. Sometimes, it may extend to a two-month credit period. You also have to help the distributor with redistribution expenses, in addition to his profit margins. The brunt of supply chain expenses, higher margins and extension of credit are squarely borne by the manufacturer. If you leave a gap anywhere, the supply to the consumer will be affected. As this cycle starts in one particular territory, you start the same cycle again in a new market where you expand. This struggle for the manufacturer is a continuous process and winning in the FMCG space in India is the biggest challenge that a business faces. That is why I compare this FMCG entrepreneurial journey to a roller coaster ride.

I have been riding this roller coaster for a long time. Sometimes, I would not participate in any social or family functions because I would be busy with my work. Many a time, I felt ashamed as I may not have had money to spend like my salaried family members or friends. I also withdrew largely because I had not achieved anything at that time and people would ridicule me for taking such a big risk to set up a business, when I had the qualification and experience to work in a multinational FMCG company. This phase is a transitory one for the person who works hard.

This roller coaster ride reminds me of the struggle of a baby giraffe to stand on its own legs when it is born. At birth, the baby giraffe falls from a height of 10 feet and rolls like a ball with its legs tucked in. The mother giraffe kicks the baby aggressively, in such a way that the baby rolls head over heels. The mother repeats her action until the baby manages to stand on its own legs! The phenomenon is driven by nature; if the mother giraffe does not do that in the forest, the baby would become a prey for other animals! Nature has its own way of giving a roller coaster ride, even to a baby giraffe, for its survival!

The most important lesson that I would like to impart is the need to sustain the success when you achieve it. I compare this to holding a tiger by the tail. If you leave it, you lose control and the tiger can kill you. You've got to hold on to the tail! Likewise, you cannot bask in the comfort of the success achieved. Once the entrepreneur becomes successful, he must not spare any effort to take the business to the next level, so that all the stakeholders of the business also continue to be successful. Most importantly, the business should have impacted customers to the extent that you have to keep serving them tirelessly, thereby raising the bar higher! There is no end to what a man can do in the FMCG business if he understands that he has committed to serve all his customers. Satisfied, happy and delighted customers will participate in a brand's success journey forever.

Turmoil is inevitable in business. Go through it and never give up, even when you are repeatedly attacked by problems. Also, remember that the life of success—that of the beautiful butterfly—must be your final vision while you go through a transformational phase. Never be deterred by or worry about the discouraging comments from those around you; they do not know about your vision. Continue to raise the bar, to sustain success. Finally, stay focused on bringing satisfaction, happiness and delight to your customers, who will participate in the journey of your success!

17

LESSONS FROM THE LARGE AND THE SMALL

Spiders, ants and elephants teach us similar lessons, although they are so different in size!

Africa fascinates me because it was there that the first humans appeared. Hence, the first stories also began here. Through these stories, the tribes of Africa taught moral values to future generations. These stories stress on the idea, 'Failures are natural in this world. So, you should boldly swim against them, without losing heart, and you will succeed in life.'

Lessons from the Simple Spider

In one of the African stories that I have read, the spider holds an important position. We often receive just a single perspective of the spider, a negative one, and, hence, are repelled by it. But, the Africans view the positive side of the spider and applaud it, saying that it teaches excellent lessons to human society.

A spider never expects help or favours from another spider.

It does its job, which is its own responsibility. It stays in its own web, never peeping into other webs or being jealous of them.

A spider builds its web, but it works without a schedule, without waiting for anyone. It never limits itself to a small web, but makes a large one. However large the web may be, the spider never compromises on the intricacies of the web. Besides being its abode, the spider's web helps it to capture its prey and protect its offspring. Scientists have found that the silk of the spider's web is the strongest natural fibre, being nearly half the strength of a steel wire of the same thickness! are envisaging a future with bulletproof vests and parachutes made of spider silk. A humble spider's web has been acknowledged to be of much greater use to mankind!

The spider has been admired since time immemorial for its perseverance. Robert Bruce, the Scottish king, learnt his leadership lessons from the spider. He persevered and won despite a number of failures, having been inspired by a spider that did not give up, finally achieving success in its seventh attempt to build a web. A leader learns from many such beings around him.

Lessons from the Hard-working Ant

Those who want to become leaders should learn from ants, which are always busy and active. Like an athlete running towards his goal, ants move in a straight line without looking back. Of course, they face obstacles on their way, but they immediately find an alternate path and resume their journey. Those who want to become leaders should follow this way of progressing. When obstacles come, they should not step back but make a slight deviation, find another way and keep travelling, keeping the focus on the goal.

Sometimes, when we see worms or insects, we don't pay much attention to them. But when we see ants, we automatically pause to watch them. They travel neatly in a single file, in a disciplined manner; they don't compete with one another and always form a queue; they don't rush ahead but progress steadily; they always work cheerfully and never expect help; they save today for what they might need tomorrow. These are the big lessons taught by the small ants.

Learning from the Mighty Elephant

Like the ants, the elephant also teaches us extraordinary life lessons. Elephants are known for living harmoniously with each other. They work together as a team, moving together to seek food and water. They even mourn together, gathering in a group to support each other. Like the elephants, team members must care for each other. They ought to communicate with each other effectively. The largest female elephant is known to lead the herd. A leader, like the elephant, must know how to look out for each member, care for one another and make sure the family and the team are well.

He who wants to become a leader ought to stand tall and learn the qualities of elephants. At the same time, one must also look at smaller creatures like the ants and learn the lessons taught by them. A leader should have the maturity to consider both the elephant and the ant as equal sources of great learning, without thinking about their size. A good leader is the one who is able to view everybody as equal, without discriminating between the big and the small, the rich and the poor and the high and the low!

A person who wants to be a leader should be a good human being. He should understand the needs of society and formulate a path to his goal by thinking innovatively. His path is entirely his own and it is he who charts the plan and method to attain the goal. He has to follow these methods and try hard to reach his goal. He may have to face many obstacles and problems. Yet, taking these as experiences, he should work tirelessly to achieve his goal.

Once he reaches his goal, he has to form a team around himself and teach them the things that he has learnt. When he shows them the way and his experience reaches many people, his goal will be strengthened even more. Eventually, a great empire is formed in this way.

A good leader is one who achieves his goal, and turns his path into one for the others, to guide them to their own goal. He who creates his path, travels on it and shows others the way to success, becomes a true leader. He who wants to become a leader, should know how to develop strategies and work tirelessly through them.

The leader in me found a clear path to follow. I, who had tasted the masalas ground by my mother's hands, discovered an opportunity to make a business out of them, in order to serve many people. I introduced novelty and freshness into all the masalas that I served to my customers. I adopted new methods to market my products and ensured that they reached the consumers. Apart from this, I also framed a distinctive motto of distribution for my products: the right ones to the right markets in the right quantities, at the right price, at the right time! I created a wonderful sales team by choosing ordinary people and making them extraordinary through training. These salespersons directly interact with everyone in the market, sell the products and obtain the opinions and views of small-scale distributors and customers. These become our lessons to improve our products and services further.

Many people plan, but when they try to implement their plans, they get dejected by the obstacles that they face. Hence, people remain the same, average and mediocre performers, without becoming leaders. Only those who resolutely overcome obstacles, find the way to become leaders.

A leader must not only show the path but also help others walk that path so that they can find success together. I lead my people by holding their hand and working along with them. While on the job, I train them and empower them with the freedom to make decisions. I do not believe in a tall hierarchical order, as I mentioned earlier.

I would like to recount a popular corporate fable about an ant and its boss, the lion. The story goes like this: Every day, a small female ant arrived at work early and started work immediately. Her production output was immense and she was happy. The boss, a lion, was surprised to see that the ant was working without supervision. He thought that if the ant could produce so much without supervision, wouldn't she produce more if she had a supervisor?

So, the lion recruited a cockroach who had extensive experience as a supervisor and who was famous for writing excellent reports. The cockroach's first decision was to set up a clocking-in attendance system. He also needed a secretary to help him write and type his reports. He recruited a spider who managed the archives and monitored all phone calls.

The lion was delighted with the cockroach's report and asked him to produce graphs to describe production rates and analyse trends so that he could use them for presentations at board meetings. So, the cockroach had to buy a new computer and a laser printer and recruit a fly to manage the IT department.

The ant, who had once been so productive and relaxed, hated this new plethora of paperwork and meetings, which used up most of her time.

The lion came to the conclusion that it was high time to put a person in charge of the department where the ant worked. The position was given to the cicada, whose first decision was to buy a carpet and an ergonomic chair for his office. The cicada also needed a computer and a personal assistant, who he had brought with him from his previous department, to help him prepare a work-and-budget control strategic optimization plan.

The department where the ant worked had now become a sad place, where nobody laughed any more and everybody was upset. It was at that time that the cicada convinced the lion to start a climatic study of the environment. Having reviewed the charges of running the ant's department, the lion found out that the production was much lower than before—so he recruited the owl, a prestigious and renowned consultant, to carry out an audit and suggest solutions. The owl spent three months in the department and came out with an enormous report, in several volumes, that concluded that 'The department is overstaffed.'

Who did the lion fire first?

The ant, of course, because 'she showed a lack of motivation and had a negative attitude.'

Layers of hierarchy mean procrastination in decision-making. I believe in adding more resourceful ants who do the job efficiently. My leadership style is one that really adds value to all the stakeholders of the organization. I reiterate that we need to look up to the traits, characteristics, values and virtues of the fauna around us. They may come in different sizes and shapes, big like an elephant or as small as an ant, but one can imbibe lessons of worthwhile leadership from them.

Chalk out the path to your goals and realize that the journey towards success would be easier if people are guided through it. Like the spider who performs its role and designs its creation, be task-oriented to achieve your goals. Work hard and focus on the job like a team of ants, as you work towards success. If you want to be a leader, be a path-breaker. Work with team members and show them the means to success. And, finally, inspire yourself by remembering that a leader's lessons may come from any little thing, even an ant or a spider!

18

SOAR TO VICTORY LIKE AN EAGLE

The quality of leadership is an important quality for any person! Today's youngsters are our country's future capital. If they inculcate individuality, leadership qualities and the ability to accomplish things without losing sight of their target, then they will be like eagles.

Learning from the Eagle

Eagles are unique. Their perspective and capability differ vastly from other birds. They soar to such great heights that other birds look up at them with wonder. They never fly with other birds—they either fly with other eagles or alone.

Youngsters should be unique like eagles. They should have soaring thoughts and act in a way that amazes others. Eagles have very sharp eyesight and can see their prey from very far away. Once they decide on the prey, they surge ahead across all obstacles and swoop down on the prey to catch it.

Like the eagle, youngsters should set a target for themselves. To attain this target, they should focus on it in such a way that others are not able to guess their next move. Like the eagle, youngsters ought to pay full attention to their goal and not be distracted by other things.

A Tamil cliché says that a lion doesn't eat grass even when famished. Similarly, even when they are hungry, eagles never consume the carcasses killed by other animals. The eagle finds its own prey and consumes it alone.

Youngsters, like the eagles, shouldn't think about enjoying the wealth and properties handed down to them by their ancestors or walk in the old paths charted by them, thus losing their individuality. They should never take a share of others' success and should instead win new things, on their own.

Like the eagles, youngsters should choose only what they need. They should never pay attention to unwanted things.

Facing Storms Like the Eagle

Usually, neither human beings nor animals enjoy storms, but eagles love them. They spread their wings wide and soar in the air, fighting against the storm. They use those stormy winds just to float around and glide.

Most people are accustomed to a monotonous, simple life without changes. They like their routine to be as normal and mundane as possible. In case they face a small hindrance or an unexpected problem, they are perplexed by it. So, when it starts drizzling as they are about to go out, they become upset with nature. Nothing is an obstacle. Everything that makes life difficult is an opportunity for us to exhibit our potential. The eagle imparts this truth to us. From the eagles, we learn that only when we have the maturity to accept struggles and adversities in life, can we achieve our goal.

Choosing a Mate Like the Eagle

Eagles can also teach lessons about love to today's young generation. Many youngsters fall in love, but very few fall in love with the awareness of their strengths and abilities. That is why love affairs end in failure. Even if they succeed in love and get married, soon, they are forced to part ways.

How do you choose a life partner for a successful life together? Let me elaborate on what the eagles teach us.

When the time comes for the male and female eagles to choose their mate, they meet each other in an area inside the forest. The female eagle picks up a small twig in her beak and starts flying high with the male eagle.

Once she goes up, she drops the twig and keenly watches if the male eagle can catch it. If he does and brings it back to her, she will do it again and again, dropping the stick and watching at what height the male eagle catches it and how he does it. This happens several times. This is a test of love. Only when the male eagle succeeds in this test, will the female mate with him.

The female eagle allows love to enter her life only after examining the male eagle's ability, sense of responsibility, presence of mind, patience, etc. Thus, eagles should make an impression on the young generation, teaching them they should not enter into hasty love affairs, but choose responsible partners by putting them through tests.

Bringing Up Their Children to Become Fine Eagles

The eagles also provide great examples about bringing up children and shaping them for the world.

Once the male eagle succeeds in the test, the male and

the female mate, after which the female prepares to lay eggs. Realizing that they need a safe place to rear their young ones, they choose a place on the top of a mountain, so that no other living beings can disturb them. The male eagle begins to build the nest; he places alternate layers of thorns and sticks and a final layer of soft grass over the bottom layers. In order to make the nest really soft, he finds bird feathers and spreads them on the nest. Two layers of thorns are placed for the safety of the eggs!

Once the eaglets emerge from the eggs, the parent eagles teach them about practical things. First, the mother eagle takes the eaglets outside their nest. The scared eaglets try to go back to the nest, again and again.

Finally, to discourage them from returning to the nest, the mother eagle plucks out the feathers and grass from the nest, leaving only the thorny layer. Now, there are no comforts in the nest and the young ones are forced to leave it. Then, the mother picks them up and drops them from the mountaintop. Terrified that their life is in danger as they do not know how to fly, the young eaglets flap their wings and cry out in alarm.

The father eagle, who watches this, catches hold of them and takes them back to the top. The mother repeats the process and, again, the father saves the young ones. Eventually, the eaglets realize that it is better to trust their wings and learn to live on their own. With this realization, they begin to move their wings and gradually learn to fly.

Most of us fail to make our children understand the hardships and difficulties of life and bring them up in comfort. These children become lazy and irresponsible as adults and become a burden on society. Parents should teach children moral values at the right age, in the right way, according to the situation. This is the lesson taught by the eagles.

Our clocks are continuously running. Day by day, we age. In our old age, we have good thoughts, but our body does not function as it did before. The eagles also teach us what we should do then.

When the eagles become old, their feathers become weak. However, they still want to soar as high as usual. But, the feeble feathers do not cooperate. At this time, the eagles go to distant places and pluck out all the feathers that hinder their flight. At one point, after plucking out all the feathers, the eagle is completely bald. Then it isolates itself and spends several days resting. As days go by, new feathers grow and, finally, the eagle emerges with renewed strength.

Like the eagles that shed their feathers in old age, we should shed undesirable thoughts and actions in our old age. Only then can we think new thoughts that are conducive to the present times. I raise my head in admiration to look at the eagle. Similarly, we should rise to a level where people will look up to us in awe!

To motivate youngsters, I have drawn an analogy from the habits of an eagle. Today's youth must be like an eagle, soaring high in thoughts and deed, while staying sharply focused on the goal.

The eagle is born to soar high. Baby eagles learn to fly the hard way, when they are pushed out of the comfort zone of the nest by the parent eagles. It would definitely be uncomfortable for humans if they are pushed out of their comfort zone very early in life, but after the initial training, it is time to soar.

I am keenly interested in the careers of youngsters. When I established the Aachi Institute of Management and Entrepreneurial Development (AIMED) in Chennai, I knew that the programme on entrepreneurship ought to have practical training in an equal measure with academic orientation. The syllabus was planned accordingly, with 50 per cent of the time to be spent on practical training in Aachi's offices, factories and sales territories, through the concept of the Work Practice School (WPS). I always want our students to realize their capabilities. I have been pushing them into the professional front while they go through their courses, unlike any other run-of-the-mill programmes. It is an accepted practice at AIMED, that its entrepreneurship training modules will have a good deal of practical, on-the-job training to sculpt students into good leaders for the future.

One must be quick to move on to higher planes of growth. For example, even before I ran out of space in my first factory in Ayanambakkam, I invested in the factory estate in Red Hills and later, in a much bigger one, in Gummidipoondi. Under normal circumstances, people tend to try and manage in the available space, but even before I reached full capacity, I planned to build manufacturing facilities with higher capacities.

In business, one ought to forge ahead of competition. I can see through competition and that stands me in good stead. I am a fighter in the market, a quality that is much needed in the FMCG space. I never shrink away from penetrating effectively to reach my primary customers, who are the distributors and retailers, and my secondary customers, who are the buyers themselves.

The eagle can fly into sunlight unlike any other bird because it is said to have two sets of eyelids, one of which is said to work like sunglasses. This special eyelid protects it from the sun's rays and therefore, it can fly directly into sunlight even when a predator is in hot pursuit. The enemy is blinded by the sun's rays and loses sight of the eagle. The very design of the eagle's eyesight makes it stay ahead in any kind of chase. Like the eagle, I am always determined to move ahead into my market territories. I nurture my spirit of seeing ahead and forging forward, while infusing all my team members with the same spirit as well.

Identify yourself only with those who can help and support you in your pursuit of success. Set yourself apart from others, with lofty thoughts and noble deeds. Never take a share of the success of others; win through your own endeavour. Like the eagle, re-energize yourself when needed, to forge ahead into the future. Do not complain when you feel threatened. In this way, you are being trained for greater achievements. Finally, forge ahead of the competition and trust that you are built uniquely.

19

FEAR OF FAILURE IS
AN IMPEDIMENT TO SUCCESS

Successful people are those who conquered the fear of failure! Quite often, questions like this are addressed to me:

'I belong to an ordinary family. I always wanted to start my own business, provide employment to others and become famous. But, whenever I try to make some effort in this direction, I lose my self-confidence and the fear of failure grips me. This ruins my efforts and prevents me from proceeding further. Can I ever become successful? How do I get rid of this fear of failure?'

To these questions, my reply is:

In my life, I have come across many people like you who have not taken a single step to fulfil their dream of becoming a businessman. I would like to cite a few examples to remove your fear of failure and strengthen your self-confidence.

Jan Koum: The Inventor of WhatsApp

Jan Koum was the son of a builder in Russia. Since his family suffered in utter poverty, without being able to afford a proper meal, he went to the USA at the age of sixteen, along with his mother.

There, he began to work as a cleaner in a grocery shop. Since his salary was not sufficient, he approached Facebook and asked for a job. He was rejected because they felt that he was not fit for a job there. For several years, he lived on the benefits handed out by the government to the poor, for which he had to stand in a queue every day. It was this Jan Koum who developed WhatsApp in 2009. After developing it for five years, he sold it for one lakh crores to the same Facebook which had earlier rejected him.

If he had feared failure and lacked self-confidence, he would have survived only on free food and we wouldn't have ever got to use WhatsApp.

Oprah Winfrey: From Rags to Riches

Oprah Winfrey was born to a maid. The family faced acute poverty, with no means to access adequate food and clothing. In fact, they had to make clothes out of the gunny bags used to carry potatoes. At the age of nine, she was molested and at fourteen she became a single mother. Soon, she lost her child. Yes, Oprah Winfrey literally spent her youth in tears. Now, she is the queen of American TV. She is a millionaire and the proprietor of a media company.

If she had lacked self-confidence and feared failure, the world would not have seen shows held by this wonderful lady.

All these are examples from other nations. There are many lessons to learn from our country, as well. There is Dhirubhai Ambani, who started his entrepreneurial stint with Rs 15,000; Narayana Murthy, who began Infosys with wife Sudha's gift of

Rs 10,000 and many others. Many friends of mine in Tamil Nadu also fall into this category.

It is possible for you to join this list pretty soon. So, get rid of your fear of failure and take your first step with confidence. Success awaits you!

Benjamin Franklin: A School Dropout

The USA acknowledges seven people as its founding fathers and one of them is Benjamin Franklin. The hundred dollar bills in the USA have carried his image for more than a century, from 1914.

Benjamin Franklin is a fine example to study. I always compare my life to his, the victim of repeated failures. Benjamin Franklin, the Father of America, was born in 1706 and lived till 1790.

'Do you want people to remember you even after your death? Either write something worth reading or do something worth writing about,' said Benjamin Franklin.

The first requirement, for writing something worth reading or doing something worth writing about, is experience! The name of the teacher who gives us this 'experience' is 'failure'. We need to make multiple efforts to obtain the experience of success. But the teacher called 'failure' comes seeking us, like a hard taskmaster. Though we may refuse to accept him, though we plead with God to stop him from entering our lives, this teacher still comes to us.

Let him come! Never chase away failure. Taste your failure. The more you taste, the more worthy your life becomes. It is failure that will make you do things that are worth writing about. You may ask, 'Wouldn't success make you write books worth reading?'

Failure and success produce two different kinds of books. Failure is a book filled with things which are of great help to others, but if you open the book called success, most of the pages are empty, with nothing printed on them. This is because most successful businessmen do not know how to explain their success. To be precise, they wouldn't know how they succeeded. It remains a mystery to them. So, they merely say that it was a blessing from God or the result of hard work, when actually it was their failures that had made them worthy of success.

That is also why failure is a printed book, so that others can read it and benefit from it. Success is not a printed book. Those who have tasted success, only they can see the cover of this book. That is why I tell you to taste failure and enjoy success.

Let me tell you how Benjamin Franklin tasted failure.

His father Josiah married twice and had seventeen children. Young Benjamin was sent to school when he was eight years old. He detested mathematics so he discontinued his studies at the age of twelve and joined a printing press run by his brother. He had the habit of reading whatever paper he could get hold of, at the press. He used to go to the harbour and plead with the sailors to lend him the books they had read.

Whether he understood them or not, he read whatever he got.

In those days, only two newspapers were published in the city of Boston. They republished the news from foreign magazines. On realizing this, Benjamin's brother decided to publish local news and he ventured into it successfully. Benjamin wanted to write articles for his brother's newspaper but he was always shooed away by his brother, who called him a fool, one had never stepped into school. Not knowing what to do, Benjamin wrote articles on women's freedom under a pseudonym, and he used to drop them at the doorstep of his brother's press. Impressed by these articles, his brother published them willingly, since they were given freely to him. In due course, these articles from an unknown writer received a warm welcome from the readers.

One day, his brother came to know the truth and called Benjamin. Assuming that he would be praised, Benjamin met him, but all he got from his brother were harsh words and a severe thrashing. An injured Benjamin then decided to run away. He was just fifteen years old.

Can you imagine how he must have felt? Through this failure, he understood the human mind. He understood the reality of relationships. He complained to his father, who washed his hands off it, saying that he would not interfere in the siblings' quarrel and left them alone.

Benjamin started visiting printing presses, looking for a job, but his brother influenced everyone, saying that he was an utter fool and ensured that he was not given employment anywhere. Thus, a series of failures faced him. Realizing that his own brother would not allow him to survive in Boston, where he had been born and brought up, he went to Philadelphia. He listed thirteen characteristics needed for success through the experiences he had gained from his failures.

1. Silence: Speak only when needed
2. Temperance: Eat only when you need to
3. Order: Let everything have a place
4. Resolution: Act firmly and cheerfully and do things without backing off
5. Industry: Work very hard
6. Frugality: Be economical in spending
7. Sincerity: Be honest in speech and deeds
8. Justice: Approach everything equally, with no bias

9. Moderation: Avoid extremes, make others understand your ideas gently and politely, without hurting anyone
10. Cleanliness: Tolerate no uncleanliness in the body, clothes or habitation
11. Tranquillity: Don't be disturbed by trifles or small accidents
12. Chastity: Do not venery but for health or offspring, never for dullness, weakness, or the injury of your own or another's peace or reputation
13. Humility: Have the quiet confidence to allow your actions to speak for themselves

He listed these qualities and also lived by them. He later penned a book titled *Poor Richard's Almanac*, which became one of the best-selling books of all times.

Money poured in; fame escalated. He was well-settled with a wife and children, but that didn't stop him from going further; he who did not want to enjoy his wealth all by himself, thought of the people of his nation. He established a hospital, library, educational institutes, an insurance company, etc., for the benefit of the people. Venturing into research, he invented many things such as the lightning rod, bifocals, the modern stove, etc. He did not patent these inventions, but made them common property for the people.

America was a colony in the 1750s. Benjamin Franklin gave a clarion call for liberty and fought for it. That was his life.

It was not success but failure that made him one of the founding fathers of America. Both failure and shame inspired him to pen the thirteen qualities through which he attained success. There is nothing after success; but there is life after failure! Those who want to enjoy success should learn to savour failure.

Flash Floods and My Lessons from Them

A flash flood is scary. When there is a sudden downpour, rivers overflow, carrying away huge boulders and uprooting large trees. The floodwater carries away everything with it.

Many forests have been lost to flash floods; many mountains have lost their rocks and boulders to flash floods; history is full of stories of flash floods that have wrecked villages and towns and washed them out to sea.

Flash floods also illustrate the difficulties faced by people who want to set up their own business. When problems crop up when we try to set up entrepreneurships, we try to take shelter under a tree or on a hill, but a flash flood of problems sweep us away along with the tree or hill.

Initially, I was caught up in such a flash flood of problems in the laundry liquid blue business. When a supplier gave me poor-quality raw materials, it resulted in a huge loss for me. Swimming hard against the flood, I managed to save myself.

When I ventured into the masala business and was moving forward step by step, I was again attacked by this vicious flood. This time, it was a real flood, as I have mentioned earlier. The Ayanambakkam Lake overflowed and flooded our factory, all our modern machines and several trucks of food products. I suffered losses to the extent of several crores of rupees at a time when I had just begun to make slow progress!

Somehow, I managed to save myself from this flood as well, when the next blow came. More than ten ingredients had to be mixed together for the chicken masala, as well as for the gobi manchurian masala. One of the ingredients was cumin seeds, which are essential for health and taste. Now, the cumin seeds had to be cleaned, ground and added to the masala mixture in the right proportion. One of our employees had been smuggling out bags of cumin seeds, which we had given him for adding to the masalas, and we were unaware of this misconduct. He had been doing this at night and this perfidy had gone on for several days. So, for a while, the masalas were prepared without the cumin seeds, packed and sent to the shops for the consumers. Later, after the customers started complaining, we came to know that the cumin seeds had not been added in the mix, as the employee had smuggled them out for his personal benefit. However, by this time, several thousand kilos of masalas had been made and were ready for sale. Immediately, we withdrew all the products from the market. Then, we set things right by adding the cumin seeds to the masalas and supplied the correct products to the shops. As a result, we faced a heavy loss once again!

However, I never thought of these flash floods of problems as failures. I savoured them and examined all the failures. In fact, these flash floods of problems taught me a formula for success.

During heavy rain, the flash flood rushes ferociously, carrying away trees, boulders and everything in its path. Similarly, when difficulties, failures and losses assail us, it seems like they are taking away everything that we have. At that moment, we should never be perturbed and think, 'Oh, I'll lose everything, I am finished!' If we falter at that moment, we will lose what we have, just like everything is carried away by the flood. But if we remain calm and confident, we will notice the trees and boulders also being carried to us by the flood.

And that's where you learn a life-saving principle: Flash floods bring along trees. Why? To save the people drowning in the water! A man caught in a flood looks out for something to hold on to, and when a tree or branch comes his way, he should understand that this is God's arrangement to save those who are drowning in difficulties. If he uses this opportunity to keep himself afloat, he can save himself from the flood.

Along with the trees, floods toss up and roll down many boulders which act like barriers to prevent us from being washed away.

Initially, I was frightened by image of the flash flood, carrying away trees and boulders; but, later, I understood that they were opportunities for me to make my escape so I learnt to use them to do so. Once I learnt this, I never worried about the flash flood of problems again.

Whenever the flash floods of problems and difficulties try to pull you down, do not lose your presence of mind. Swim against the flash flood with confidence. Hold on to the things that keep you afloat and bring you respite. Wrestle with the flood with a fighting spirit, and make sure that you do not drown or suffocate. Like me, you too will surely come out of it, clinging onto a tree or blocked by a piece of rock. You too will succeed!

The flash floods of problems can wipe away the efforts made over the years. I faced a similar plight when my factory was inundated and when a miscreant stole an ingredient. Events like these could have an appalling effect not only on the product but also on the brand. I had the presence of mind to immediately call back the substandard products. Many others would have let it go. My conscience did not let me sell a substandard product to customers, even though I faced a huge loss. When problems strike repeatedly, they may wash away our efforts, but we should not let them wash away our dreams. I am someone who has never let such failures wash away my dream of success.

Calamities may land one in deep trouble. I always love to share the achievements of people who have really fought hard in life to win over odds. I recollect a conversation I recently had with my friend Gibson about a winning personality in our living room as we were watching TV. Even when we stayed in a small house, we would not let Gibson stay in a hotel when he visited Chennai. Now, it has become routine to have him stay in one of our guest rooms when he visits Chennai. We watch TV, especially just after dinner. In the serial that we were watching one evening, the popular Indian actress and danseuse Sudha Chandran came on screen. I looked at him and asked (it is my habit to quiz him on interesting happenings and current news), 'Did you know that this beautiful lady does not have a leg and yet she dances so gracefully?' He said, 'Yes, I know.' I told him how she had lost a leg at sixteen, when a neglected wound became infected, eventually resulting in amputation. Well, Gibson had not been aware that she had lost a leg in the prime of her youth until I told him about it. I spoke of the pain she must have gone through, especially as a dancer. I urged him to think of the determination with which she fought back and the numerous obstacles she would have overcome to dance again, so beautifully, as a professional dancer. I told him how she must have faced great pain when she practised dancing or when she rehearsed as an excellent actress! I reminded him that it must have taken much more time and skill for her, compared to an able-bodied person, to perform so well—so great was her determination to succeed against circumstances. Many others in similar circumstances would have lost hope and sought the sympathies of people around them but she was determined to succeed. Our failures in business are nothing compared to what Sudha Chandran has gone through. Hats off to her!

I exercise an empathetic way of truly understanding the life of another successful person, especially to know how much pain lay behind the success. I thought about the pain and the problems that Sudha Chandran would have borne while she tried to attain the pinnacle of success. She faced painful physical challenges and worked on them continuously to achieve great success. I not only hold Sudha Chandran in very high esteem, but I also recognize what we can learn from her. I have a special place for her in my list of celebrated achievers!

Fear of failure can destroy your self-confidence. Once you set up a business, do not think that it is going to be a bed of roses. Be prepared to face problems and failures. Consider failures as temporary setbacks that can be removed if you persistently work on solutions. When calamities strike, they can do so with the intensity of flash floods, wiping away all your efforts. Hold on to your dream of achievement and work harder to stay afloat. Keep in mind that failures are the pages of the book of your experience. Learn from experiences to excel better than before. Renew and rebuild what has been lost, without brooding on the things that have been lost. And, finally, if you learn to enjoy failures, you will treat them as stepping stones to a successful future.

20

YOU DESERVE YOUR SUCCESS: ENJOY IT!

Setting up or running a business is not a bed of roses!
An entrepreneur's business journey is often a wild path filled
with stones and thorns. It is a narrow track where a misstep
can topple you into deep gorges. Yet, youngsters who wish to
become successful entrepreneurs should not be intimidated
by these things; they should not lose heart on encountering
problems. Nobody achieves anything easily and, if they do, the
world doesn't consider it an achievement, but something that
has happened by fluke.

Some Dos and Don'ts for Businessmen

Don't perceive things in the same way as others do. If everyone
who sees a rose complains that God has made it with so many
thorns, you should say, 'I adore God who has put the rose in
the midst of thorns!'

Don't be dejected when the door of opportunity is half-
closed. Rather, be happy that the other half is still open and
plan your strategy to enter through the half-open door. Learn

to perceive things positively.

Society does not welcome all those who want to establish businesses. Entrepreneurs are often criticized for giving up well-paying jobs and taking a big risk to set up businesses. The common thought in people's minds is that they may not succeed. This kind of negativity is unavoidable because people may not be aware of what you want to do and how you want society to benefit from your venture. You have to prove yourself to society by delivering benefits through your business, by virtue of its product or service portfolio, resulting in the economic upliftment of society and the nation. Instead of complaining about the lack of a welcome, help society enjoy the benefits that your business can bring. If you do that, society will give you a warmer reception than you ever expected. The successful formula is very simple: The benefit you give to society through your business, should be more than your profit. Those who offer such benefits to society, have turned out to be successful businessmen. While technology companies aim to bring in more enterprise efficiency and increase productivity, a food manufacturer like me offers healthy, tasty and nutritious products that enhance the quality of people's lives, especially those of women. Everyone who starts a business should focus on the kind of products that can directly benefit the people being served. Those who make such products and render such services would be welcomed warmly.

The best charity in this world is given through food. The noblest service in the world is farming. Both are related to nourishment. Food can weave itself into man's feelings and life; it is divine. That is why I ventured, wholeheartedly, into the food product business. Today, I don't see it as a business. I am doing this as a divine service and as a service to society. More than the money, it is the goodwill of the people that stands me in good stead. I feel contentment in my soul. Through this business, I am fulfilling the great commission entrusted to me by God, who is accomplishing the purpose of my birth.

Be a Merchant Seeking Pearls

Whenever I open the Bible, my eyes fall on the verse, 'The kingdom of Heaven is like a merchant seeking beautiful pearls!' These lines touch my heart. I love people, beyond religion. At the same time, I am astounded by the honour given to merchants in the Bible, and I feel blessed by this. I wish that all the businessmen who work for our society should feel similarly blessed.

Why should we taste failure and enjoy success? Why should failure be tasted? We should, at the outset, know the difference between tasting and relishing. When we taste our favourite dish, all our five senses are involved. Only when we taste something, do we think deeply and clearly about it.

Similarly, with failure, only when we accept it and taste it, can we analyse it clearly and move on to the next level. Analysis is essential for discovering the reason behind the failure and to avoid similar situations in future.

I have tasted many failures and, in doing so, tried to ensure that I would not fail again. You should also taste it boldly and share its taste with others. It would show the way to many people and teach them how to face failure and overcome it.

Relish Success Like an Emperor

You may ask why success should be enjoyed.

Yes, learn to relish success, as a hard-working ant finally relishes the food it gathers. Tasting failure is beautiful, for you gain experiences and learning through it. Enjoying success is like reaping the harvest of those failures.

Finally, I would like to conclude with a story, one that reveals a great truth.

An emperor from the Qin dynasty ruled over a great empire. The neighbouring kings admired him for his golden rule, but the king had no peace of mind and, therefore, no rest. Day after day, he felt burdened by a heavy load of worries. At that time, a Zen Master, who was a scholar, visited the country. The king met him and asked him to show the way to attain peace. After asking him several questions, the Master found out the actual reasons for the king's lack of peace.

'You say that you are mentally burdened; so, it is better if you hand over this country to me!'

'Okay. Take it from me ...'

'What would you do if you gave me this country?'

'I would take some money for my journey and go to an unknown place.'

'If you give me the country, your treasury too, would belong to me. Then, you don't have the right to take any money...'

'What you say is correct. So, I would go with what I have and work somewhere for my living...'

'Let me give you an idea! Be my representative and take care of the kingdom until I return. Take your salary from the treasury. Keep a clear account.'

'Good idea! I will follow your instructions.'

He did so and acted as the representative of the Master, who came back after a few years. The Master asked the king with a smile, 'Do you feel peaceful now?'

The king said, 'Yes, I am so peaceful now.'

'How did you find peace?'

'I have no idea...'

'What is the difference between ruling the country as the king and ruling it as my representative?'

'Nothing special! It's the same palace; the same officers; the same method of ruling; but, at that time, I had no peace. Now, I am peaceful. I don't understand the reason; please tell me,' he humbly asked the Master.

'At that time, you thought, "This is my country."And now, instead of that, you think, "This country belongs to someone else; I am a mere representative. This does not belong to me." With this thought, all your burdens and sorrows have left.

'This world is not ours. Who created it? Your body doesn't belong to you! Your fame is not yours. Who has given this to us? With this thought, carry out your duties and you will not feel worried or burdened by troubles any more!'

This is an excellent principle for life. Don't feel proud that all your successes belong to you—your burden will only increase and your happiness will dwindle. We should move away from thinking, 'Me! This belongs to me.' Instead, if we develop the broad perspective of, 'My success is for the people and for society,' we would perform every good deed for society and when we do so, sorrow will flee and peace will enter our lives!

Read this story at least three times. Think about this at least thirty times. Live your life according to it. You will attain peace and, when we are at peace, we can impart the same to those around us. When everyone is at peace, prosperity and joy will be there in the country. Let us live for the nation and its people. Let us forget ourselves and learn to love others, unconditionally! And, all the peace and joy that come with success, will be added unto us.

The life of an entrepreneur is one of turmoil and hard

work, very different from that of an employee who works for an organization. There are many people in an existing organizational system and there are defined processes in an organization. Responsibilities and accountabilities are shared and goals are subsequently achieved. These are organizations that have come a long way from the initial stages of the growth cycle. For an entrepreneur, everything is done step by step; the owner has to toil alone for many months and, sometimes, yearns for a team to help him out. The initial days are harder as there might be only a few companions to work with, sharing your vision. So, when working with a team of people who have well-defined roles, ensuring responsibilities and deliverables is much easier, whereas working to fulfil a dream with few resources is an uphill task. In addition to the multifarious functional roles that the entrepreneur has to perform, there are a plethora of setbacks and failures that he may face. Immunity against odds is built in business only when one suffers the various stages of this malady. That immunity becomes the platform for building a robust business and emerging sustainable and successful.

Enjoying success is different from finding happiness. Happiness is a transitory state of mind that can be found by anyone in a particular environment or in a given situation. The story of happiness lying right there at the feet of a man who is fishing on a beach, without him having to do anything, tells us that chasing happiness is futile when happiness can be found by someone doing nothing but fishing peacefully! The question then is, 'Why should anyone work on one's own business, find success and then be happy?'

The enjoyment of success is quite different from the happiness referred to in the story of the happy man on the beach. The joy that success begets is a lasting one. That joy is derived from chasing an idea, giving shape to it, making it work, rendering it useful to people and contributing to the success and happiness of people who work with you! What success brings, in this case, is the joy of building your creation. It is like seeing light at the end of a tunnel. Imagine how Neil Armstrong must have felt as he set foot on the moon! Many fears, including for his life, must have crowded his mind. But the crew made it after all their efforts and accomplished the lofty goal. As he set foot on the moon, he said, 'This is one small step for man but one giant leap for mankind.' He knew that he had created history for mankind.

Many of us know the success story of Thyrocare. The company's founder, Dr A. Velumani went to Mumbai to earn a living, with just Rs 500 in his pocket. He worked in the area of thyroid biochemistry research at the Bhabha Atomic Research Centre (BARC), Mumbai, for fifteen years before he set up his first thyrocare testing centre in 1995. His aim was to ensure that the right value is given at the right time to the right patient in the test they performed every day. His lofty vision was that, 'Thyrocare should serve 50 per cent of the world's population, 50 per cent of their diagnostic needs, at 50 per cent of the costs. The company should be the biggest client for the top twenty diagnostic manufacturing companies across the globe.' His vision has gone global, crossing Indian shores, after its success in the last two decades. In 2017, when the company was listed on the National Stock Exchange, it was subscribed over seventy-four times, creating history in the healthcare segment. That is the joy of success he created. It was at a time when he did not need money, but he bargained enough with the suitors to seek a favourable amount for the company, putting his own price on the company's valuation. Every time Mr Velumani could reduce the cost for his ultimate customers (patients), he was filled with a sense of happiness that he was serving the masses; this, combined with the good returns that he reaped on scaled-up revenues, was a double whammy!

My ambitions and thought processes are similar—to provide the masses, especially the people at lower economic levels, with products at very affordable prices. My business now gives me the enjoyment of employing people and serving people! I am proud of my hard work. Till today, I have not diluted the ownership of my company for a private investor, having found no need for it, as the company is well-funded by internal accruals and bank funding. I would divest only through an initial public offering (IPO), at the right time. My happiness and enjoyment are found in those exclusive people I added value for, as I built the organization: my distributors, retailers, factory employees, field employees and my customers! My enjoyment spills over when I see my products on the shelves of retail shops, both in India and abroad! My workers are amazed by the way I encourage them like a friend, patting them on their shoulders; students are enthralled by merging their expectations with my ideas and seeing me as their mentor; my experiences may guide businessmen towards success; I feel honoured when I receive appreciation from my customers and when women appreciate me for moving them away from the confinements of the kitchen. Through Aachi, I know that people will continue to identify me as the one who has 'individuality and paramount leadership quality'.

That sums up everything about the enjoyment of my success, as a lasting phenomenon for posterity and as an impetus carry forward in our lives!

Think differently from common perspectives. Your own point of view will pave the way for success. The role of a businessman is described as a merchant seeking pearls (and equated to the Kingdom of Heaven in the Holy Scripture). If you play that role sincerely, success will follow. Nurture this thought, as it will lead you to success: 'What you create as a business is not for yourself or for your family. It is for people and society.' Build a sustainable model of business with people and for people; it would see lasting success and the valuation of your creation will keep increasing. Finally, remember that success is for you to enjoy and to spread that enjoyment over the future by passing it on for posterity!

ACKNOWLEDGEMENTS

When I look back, I realize that I have come a long way. In my sales career, which I began immediately after college, I learned from everyone that I interacted with. The most important of them were my distributors, who represented the company I worked for in the late 1970s through to the 1980s. I am so thankful to them; they all had a deep business sense that percolated into me and motivated me to begin my own business journey.

The next set of influencers was the retailers I met day in and day out, as part of my daily routine. They were hard workers, getting up very early every morning, travelling quite a distance to procure products for their stores and tactfully convincing their customers to always buy what they had to sell. I am grateful to these retailer friends, from whom I learnt the art of understanding customers.

The consumers of Aachi products, my customers, most of them women, are my teachers in this food business. Their rejections, affirmations and feedback have, time and again, told me the most significant things I had to absorb, to be finally accepted into their households. My special thanks are due to them. They are the ones who drive all of us at Aachi, to find many tasty recipes. Without them, I would not have had failures to relish and successes to enjoy.

I would not have been able to create a business without the roles that all our business stakeholders played, right from the initial days of my business. Our colleagues and our sales and distribution people, besides our vendors, creditors, bankers, friends, our advertising and media partners and our technologists, have been the pillars of Aachi's success. I cannot find words to sufficiently express my gratitude to them.

I owe my obligations to my wife Thelma; my sons, Ashwin and Abishek; and daughters-in-law, Shiny Ashwin and Rebekah Abishek, who inspired me to write this book.

My belief in the divine power of God goes beyond religions. And to God be all the glory!